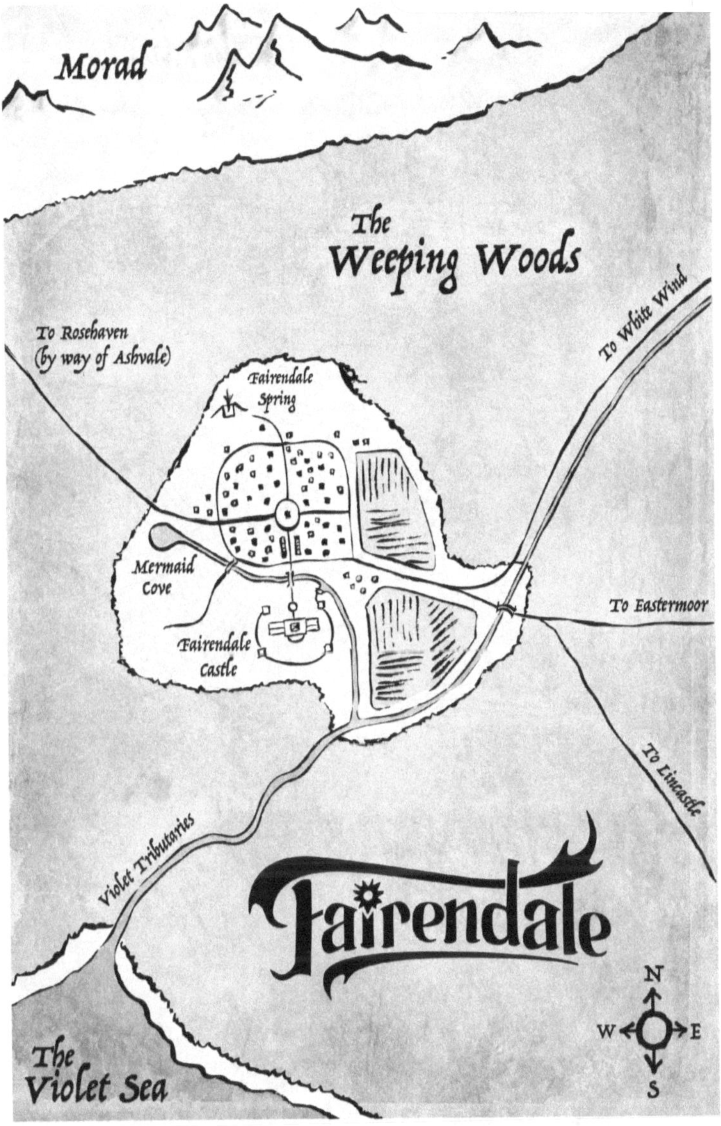

Morad
The Weeping Woods
To Rosehaven
(by way of Ashvale)
To White Wind
Fairendale Spring
Mermaid Cove
To Eastermoor
Fairendale Castle
To Lincastle
Violet Tributaries
Fairendale
The Violet Sea
N
W E
S

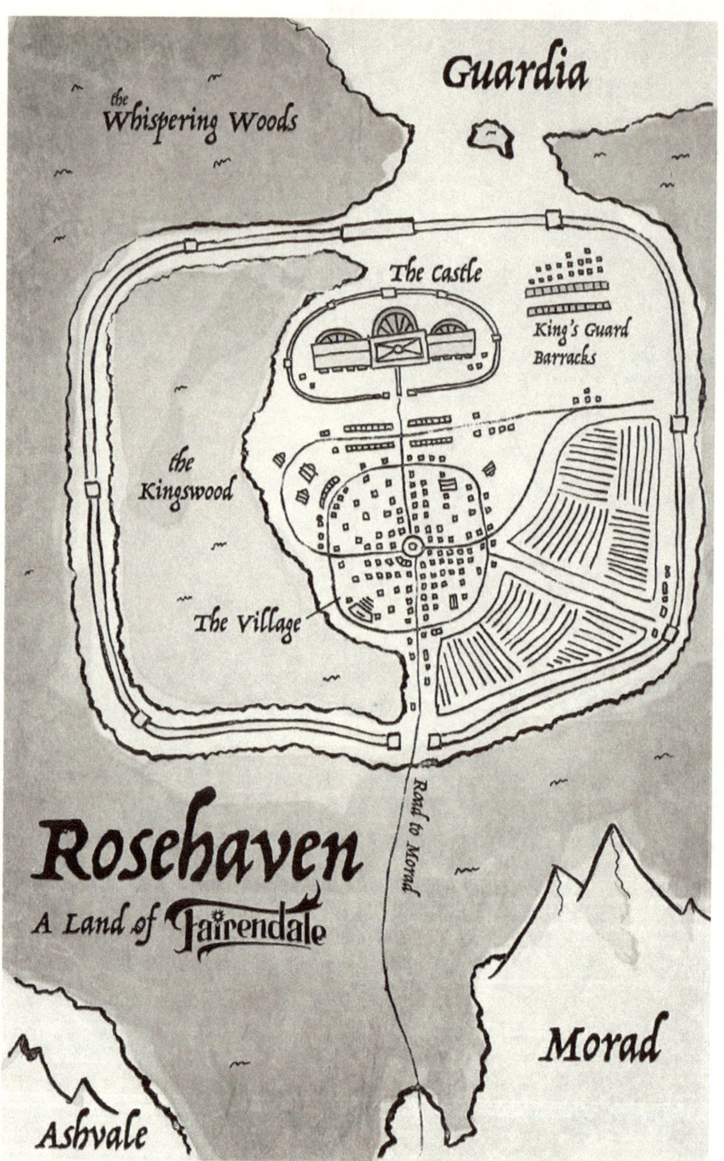

Guardia
the Whispering Woods
The Castle
King's Guard Barracks
the Kingswood
The Village
Road to Morad
Rosehaven
A Land of Fairendale
Morad
Ashvale

Fairendale

II

THE
GIRL WHO BUILT
THE TOWER

Read all the books in the Fairendale series!

Book .5: *The Good King's Fall (a prequel novella)*
Book 1: *The Treacherous Secret*
Book 2: *The King's Pursuit*
Book 3: *The Perilous Crossing*
Book 4: *The Dragons of Morad*
Book 5: *The Fiery Aftermath*
Book 6: *The Mysterious Separation*
Book 7: *The Boy Who Spun Gold*
Book 8: *The Boy Who Robbed the Rich*
Book 9: *The Girl Who Awakened the Beast*
Book 10: *The Boy Who Became the Wolf*

Collector's Editions:
Books 1-6: *The Flight of the Magical Children*

To see all the books L.R. Patton has written, please click or visit the link below:
www.lrpatton.com/writing

L.R. PATTON

THE GIRL WHO BUILT THE TOWER

BATLEE PRESS

Batlee Press
PO Box 591596
San Antonio, TX 78259

Copyright ©2018 by L.R. Patton
All rights reserved.
No part of this book may be reproduced or transmitted in any form or by any means, electronic or mechanical, including photocopying and recording, or by any information storage and retrieval system, without permission in writing from the publisher. For information regarding permission, write to Batlee Press, PO Box 591596, San Antonio, TX 78259.

The author appreciates your taking the time to read her work. Please consider leaving a review wherever you bought it and telling your friends how much you enjoyed it. Both of those help get the book into the hands of new readers, which is incredibly important for authors. Thank you for your support.
www.lrpatton.com

This is a work of fiction. Names, characters, places and incidents are either the product of the author's imagination or are used fictitiously, and any resemblance to actual persons, living or dead, business establishments, events or locales is entirely coincidental.

Printed in the United States of America

First Edition—2018/Cover designed by Toalson Marketing
www.toalsonmarketing.com

To B.A.T.
You are kind, you are careful, you are noble.
You will grow a wondrous garden.

Decisions

Fairies. A whole line of them, inside a shelter in the woods near Lincastle, where August and the other lost boys of Fairendale stand, open-mouthed, vacillating between two options: Run? Remain?

No one has ever outrun a fairy. The boys are, to be quite honest, terrified of fairies. The stories of Fairendale tell of fairies who, in moments of rage or curiosity—whatever moves a fairy to act—snatch up children and take them to a land where they never grow up. On days when the parents of Fairendale enacted some ridiculous rule or expectation, the children of Fairendale paged through the stories and imagined they were already residents of the land without parents. Permanent residents. But it never took them long to remember that they loved their parents very much, and they would likely miss those parents terribly if they never got to see them again. Ever.

August and the lost boys have already spent far too many days outside the presence of their mothers and fathers and brothers and sisters, and not only do they miss their families terribly, but they would like to one day see them again—which means the fairies pose a significant threat, if the stories they have heard are true.

"The magic must have worn off," August says to himself. Leo hears him and looks at him with questioning eyes. August does not explain that their friend Theo covered the shelter in a Protection spell days ago, before leaving them so he could turn himself over to the king of Fairendale, who pursues all the lost children of the land, searching for a magical boy.

Theo was the magical boy.

Theo is still gone.

August tries not to allow himself to think of the implications of Theo's continued absence and the presence of these fairies. The Protection spell is no longer working. Theo has not returned. What if the king of Fairendale has executed August's best friend?

He shakes his head to clear it as best he can. He must concentrate on the situation at hand. Hundreds—or could it be thousands?—of fairies glow in the shadows of the shelter. The boys have not said a word.

"Hello boys," says one fairy in a voice that sounds like tiny bells tinkling. August wonders if she is the leader of the throng. Do fairies have leaders? "What are you doing in the middle of our forest?"

She glides closer to them, on opaque green wings. She is dressed in a silken red gown that reaches her ankles. The sleeves are bell-shaped, like a royal gown in miniature. Her hair is golden and pinned to the top of her head. Her eyes are deep green, like the lacy leaves of the forest trees.

"Do not come near us," August says. They are the only words he can think to say, so tongue-tied is he.

The fairy laughs, a ringing sound in the otherwise quiet of the shelter. "As you wish," she says, and she hovers, her wings moving so rapidly they are green blurs.

But another fairy, this one bright pink with a yellow dress that looks much like the first fairy's in its extravagance, flits about between the boys. They lean back and then forward, trying to escape the incessant buzzing in their ears.

"Enough, Misha," the green fairy calls out in a sharp voice. "Return to your rank."

The pink fairy obeys, and the green fairy folds her tiny hands together in front of her. "Now, then," she says.

"My question. I do not believe you answered it."

August merely stares at the fairy. He is unsure what to do. Should he answer the question? Should he ignore it altogether?

"Perhaps it would be easier for you if you knew my name," she says, her voice softening into threads of silk. "I am Tara, a leader of the fairies. Not the ruler"—and here her face pinches slightly, but then she smoothes it into a smile—"but a leader." The mass of fairies glows slightly brighter. They are beautiful—small pinpoints of light in every color and hue.

Not one of the boys offers his name.

"There is a boy who left you," Tara says. "You do not know if he is coming back."

"He is coming back," August says, before he can stop himself.

"You have much faith in him," Tara says. "Faith would be good to have in our land. Loyalty, too." She looks at them, an invitation in her voice. "You are welcome there."

"We will not leave," August says. "Theo told us to remain in this shelter until he returned. And so we will remain." His voice, much to his frustration, has grown slightly weaker in the moments since meeting these fairies. His words sound eloquent enough, but they lack conviction.

The fairy smiles. "And so," she says. She looks at August. He is unable to look away. Her voice stretches across the distance. "We come from a lovely land. I believe you would enjoy it there."

"We will never go," August says. His voice cracks now.

"In this place, boys never grow old," Tara says. "They remain in their best form: children."

"And why would we want to remain children?" Leo says from behind August, near the right wall. August is grateful for his intervention. Leo's voice, too, lacks conviction, but his words strengthen all the others. August can feel it in the way they straighten their backs and breathe more evenly.

The fairy gazes past August. Her smile widens. "Why, because you do not need to grow up in Never Land. Everything is provided for you. It is a simple, extraordinary life."

The boys lean forward. August clears his throat.

"We are uninterested," he says.

The fairy tilts her head, her green eyes flashing. "And why would you want to stay in this land?" she says, extending her arms in a half-moon. She lets them drop again.

"It is our home," August says.

"This is not your home," Tara says. "Your home no longer exists."

The boys suck in their breaths. August can feel their hesitation pressing on his shoulders.

"Some of you lost your parents in the king's…" Here Tara pauses. She seems to find what she desires and finishes: "War." She lets the word dangle like it wears wings of its own. "Many of you will lose more in what is coming."

"What is coming?" Leo says. There is no longer enough light to see his face, but August can hear the tremor in his voice.

"Many horrible, unspeakable things," Tara says. "Or so we have heard."

The words dance upon the air inside the shelter. They skip across the faces of the boys. They lodge into their chests in precisely the right way, spilling doubt into the depths of every boy present. The room tilts slightly in front of August. He presses his hand against the wall.

"We could protect you," Tara says. She has drawn closer without August even noticing. "We could take you to our land, and what is coming could not touch you."

The fairies glow brighter all around them, casting the shelter in many colors. It is warm and lovely and smells of honey and nectar. The boys do not answer. August considers.

But, in the end, he says, "We shall remain," and the breaths of the boys behind him release as one.

Tara balls her fists and moves closer to August. He leans back, pressing against the boy behind him. "You will never make it out alive, boy," she says. "Who is it you think has been protecting this shelter from all the forest's monsters?"

A hiss sounds from outside the structure. August's heart whirls inside his chest. "Theo," he says.

The fairy laughs, and the rest of them laugh along with her. It is a tinkling song that is frightening, not comforting. "The magical boy," Tara says. "He is no longer here. How would he protect you now?"

August does not know the answer to this question, but he cannot tell the fairy this. So he says, "Theo's magic is strong. Strong enough to be a king."

He feels the stillness of the boys behind him. The boys, with the exception of Fineas, did not know that Theo possessed the gift of magic. Theo's secret is out. But it was for a good and noble cause, August tells himself.

"The fairies have been protecting you, foolish boy," Tara says. "But now I am afraid we must leave you to your fate." She turns toward the fairies, her wings carrying her gracefully back to their line.

"Wait," Fineas says. The fairy turns around, and she is smiling.

"We do not need the help of fairies," August says. But Fineas pushes past him, into the center of the shelter, which takes only two steps.

"Perhaps we might think about it," Fineas says.

"Ah," Tara says. "I see that not all of you are as foolish as that one." She points a tiny finger at August and then fixes her eyes on Fineas. "Three days," she says. "I shall give you three days to think about it."

"And you will protect us?" Fineas says.

Tara smiles. "Of course," she says. "And all you have to do when you would like me to return is call my name. All you have to do to live in a land that is more wonderful than you can possibly imagine is say, 'We would like to come with you to Never Land.'" She looks at each of the boys in turn. Her gaze lingers on August. "Do not be foolish enough to wait on someone who will never return."

And with that she is gone and the rest of the fairies with her. In the corner, where they fanned out in their colorful line, is a gift of bread. Many loaves of bread. The boys give a cry, push toward the corner, and set upon eating it.

Only August hesitates. Only August watches the window through which the fairies departed. Only August turns the words over and over in his mind, folds them up, and tucks them in a corner of his heart, for another day.

Someone who will never return.

He will not wait forever.

It is another early morning, the sacred moments before the sun rises and spills into the easternmost window of the cottage where the three Graces—Good Cheer, Mirth, and Splendor—reside. Every morning, at exactly this time, they pull out their magical looking ball, which is a permanent fixture, covered by a green cloth, in the corner of their sitting room. It is a ritual: the Graces lift the cloth every morning and gaze into the ball, where they will meticulously eye every corner of the realm, checking for the manifestation of darkness, and, if or when they locate it, determining whether it is time for them to intervene or simply continue waiting for the natural eradication of darkness by the people who interact with it. Sometimes the people are not strong enough. Sometimes they are not wise enough. Sometimes they simply do not notice darkness, for one reason or another.

The Graces are gifted with the powers of inexhaustible magic of every kind—including Vanishing spells in which they reappear in their original form, which allows them to travel quickly across long distances and time their intervention to the perfect moment. They are given authority to change the trajectory of fate, if they so desire it. They are permitted to use magic however and whenever they want—they can create something from nothing if circumstances call for it. In other words, the Graces break every magical rule of this land.

There are two powers, however, that are denied them: that of taking another life or raising it from the dead and that of Seeing the future. Their ball only shows them what is happening in the present moment. This means that intervening is somewhat complicated. They never know how their intervention will turn out, and so they will consider it from every possible angle before they move to act. Still, even though they consider it from every possible angle, sometimes they are quite surprised by how well or how badly they alter fate.

Good Cheer wriggles her fingers above the ball, and it glows green. She scans through the lands quickly, until she reaches the woods to the south, between Lincastle and Fairendale. "Well," Good Cheer says, and the others lean closer. "There is a monster loose in the area." Her dark eyes narrow. She presses a hand the shade of milky chocolate to the collar of cream-colored pearls that wrap her neck, as she tends to do when she is disturbed by something. This causes the other two Graces to draw closer to her.

"She is the one who will bring about the destruction?" Splendor says. Her blue-green eyes blink rapidly.

"If you believe what we have been told," Good Cheer says. "Then yes."

The room in which they stand is a curious one. There are places to sit, of course, for this is a sitting room, but the furniture is not what one would notice upon first entering the room. One would likely notice the paintings on the walls. There are sorcerers and sorceresses of varying sizes and ages and magical ability painted into every frame that hangs on the walls. The sorcerers and sorceresses are currently still, in painted poses, but what is rather strange is that between the hours of sundown and sunup, these painted portraits move and talk and sometimes even disappear.

The green light of the ball illuminates the faces of

the Graces, casting them in an other-worldly glow, which makes them appear as though they are not entirely human. And, in fact, they are *not* entirely human—they have died and risen again to become the watchers of the realm, the Protectors of the seven kingdoms, the Graces of mirth, splendor, and good cheer for all people, everywhere.

"We must begin our work soon," Good Cheer says.

Mirth claps her hands. "At last," she says. "We shall be needed."

Good Cheer glares at her. "We are always needed."

Mirth rearranges the smile on her face and presses a hand against Good Cheer's arm. "That is not what I meant."

"I know," Good Cheer says. Her shoulders slump slightly. It is unusual to see her in such a posture, and it disturbs the other two Graces.

"What is it?" Splendor says.

"It will not be easy," Good Cheer says. "We must take care."

"As we always do," Splendor says.

"We have never been needed like this," Good Cheer says. "We must fold the right edges, empower the right people, press light into the right places."

"We have been given this power because we are

worthy," Splendor says. She lifts her chin. Her orange-red hair falls across one shoulder in shining waves. "Because we have been chosen."

"We have never encountered a creature like this one," Good Cheer says. "One so full of darkness."

"But we are full of light," Mirth says. "And light is always enough to cast out the darkness."

"She will have the help of the darkest creatures in the forest," Good Cheer says.

"And the people will have our help," Mirth says.

Good Cheer turns her eyes away from the ball, and it flickers into a clear glass sphere and nothing more. Splendor replaces the green cloth, hiding the ball once more. Mirth takes Good Cheer's hand and leads her to a chair. Without a word, she prepares a cup of tea, without cream or sugar, just as Good Cheer prefers it. She sets it on the table. Steam rises from the blue ceramic teacup. Mirth follows the winding trail with her eyes until it dissipates into nothing.

"Sit," Good Cheer says, and Mirth sits, along with Splendor, who joins them with a smile.

"Tell us what troubles you," Mirth says, for it is clear that Good Cheer has not yet told them everything.

Good Cheer shakes her head. She looks at each of them in turn. "What we must do involves your families," she says. "We must make the right decision regardless."

Mirth and Splendor exchange a look, and then they nod. "Of course," they say. "We are Graces."

Mirth reaches for Good Cheer's hand across the table. "And your family?" she says. "What of them?"

Good Cheer drops her eyes to the cup and withdraws her hand from beneath Mirth's, presumably to lift the teacup with two hands rather than one. She sips and sets the cup back down. She does not speak for some time. At last she says, "My family, what is left of it, will be affected as well."

And Mirth and Splendor feel less alone.

But then a shadow crosses Mirth's face. "Were we not supposed to forget our families?" she says. Good Cheer and Splendor make a small sound in the backs of their throats. Mirth stares at them. "I remember mine."

"I remember mine as well," Splendor says. "My sons." Her voice cracks.

"It is a trick," Good Cheer says. "It is a way to set us on the wrong trail."

"But who would have done this?" Mirth says. "The monster in the woods?"

"No," Good Cheer says. "It is much too complicated for her kind of magic." She stares at her hands, wrapped around the cup. "It was the Grim Reaper. He is the only one who could gain from our misstep. He is diverting our attention elsewhere."

They all stare at the table, silently considering the implications of such a thing.

"We must forget," Good Cheer says. Her eyes lift to her sisters. "We must do it for one another."

"A Memory Extraction spell?" Splendor says. A crease forms between her perfect eyebrows.

"Yes," Good Cheer says. She touches the pearls at her neck. "We must. It is the only way."

"Very well, then," Mirth says, though it is not without much sorrow that she stands. "Let us do it right away."

"But first," Good Cheer says, and she moves from the table, down the hallway to her room. She emerges with a small, round pot with purple flowers painted all over it.

"What is that?" Mirth says.

"It is a Morari," Good Cheer says. "A place where memories go." She touches the pearls around her neck, and they become a long, white staff in her left hand. "We will bid our memories to gather in this pot, so we will always have them should we need them."

Mirth and Splendor nod. And then they all stand, in the circle mandated by the table. They begin the incantation, Good Cheer touching Mirth, who touches Splendor, who touches Good Cheer. And when the incantation has wrapped them in a cold green mist, they feel their memories lift, spin, and vanish. The pot on the table clatters for a moment before its lid slams.

When they are finished, they do not remember why they stand. Mirth returns to the iron stove, where she will set a kettle to boil, pour the water over leaves, and hand Good Cheer another cup of tea. Good Cheer will drink it, and Splendor will drop into a chair, and the Graces will sit, talking about the fine day that is unfolding outside the kitchen window.

Cook, the cook from Fairendale castle who is currently enrobed in her bear skin, looks in on the Graces. They do not see her standing at the window, peering in at them, but if they did, they would be able to tell, almost immediately, that there is something different, something strange about this brown bear. She has a body that belongs to an animal and yet eyes that belong to a human—rich brown ones that sparkle and shine. Intelligent eyes, some might call them. She takes in the scene before her with these intelligent, human eyes, knowing that she must not disturb it. But when the Graces return the scrap of cloth to the looking ball, concealing it once more, Cook lumbers to the front door, waits several moments—perhaps even hours; for a bear, time does not have the same linear shape it wears for a human—and scratches on it with a large and somewhat awkward paw.

The Grace with orange-red hair opens the door. She says to the others, "The bear has returned."

Cook is startled. She has been here only once, weeks ago, but she thought she had not been seen.

"We did see you, bear," says the red-haired Grace. "We see everything. We are the Protectors of the realm."

So Cook stands to her full height, on two feet. If they are all-knowing, they must know she can speak.

"Why have you come to us?" says the brown-skinned Grace.

"I come to request help for Fairendale," Cook says. Her voice, as a bear, rumbles and growls. It is most unlike her voice as Cook. It amuses her every time. She chokes on a chuckle.

The dark-skinned grace tilts her head. "Why?" she says.

"Because it is the land I love," Cook says. "And it is the land I have been given to restore."

The Graces stare at her for a moment. They look at each other and then back at her. "The land you have been given to restore?" says the dark-skinned one.

"Yes," Cook says.

"And by whom have you been given this order?" says the dark-skinned Grace.

Cook considers this. Bregdon, perhaps? He is the one who summoned her. But who is he in the realm? She has not been able to figure this out. In fact, she has not seen him in many years. She says, "I am a shape shifter," as though this might explain something.

And perhaps it does. The Graces look at one another. The brown-haired one says, "A shape shifter."

"The time has almost come," says the brown-skinned one. She looks back at Cook. "You will join our cause." It is not a question.

Cook bows slightly. "I already have," she says. "This spinning wheel—"

"We must add one more to the count," says the red-haired Grace. Her eyes flash at Cook, as though Cook has said words that should not be said.

"Go and meet your people," says the brown-skinned Grace. "And when we need you, we will call."

Cook nods and returns to all fours. She has already met two of her people. Who are the others? She hesitates before saying, "Two of my people helped me hide the spinning wheel."

The brown-skinned Grace holds up her hand. Her eyes flash. "We must not speak of a spinning wheel."

And Cook knows, with a great rush of warmth, that she and the others were sent by the Graces to take care of this magical spinning wheel. To hide it. Of course the Graces already know it is buried beneath the Great Tree of Helomoth.

She feels foolish for having brought it up. She turns toward the woods.

"Wait." The red-haired Grace's voice turns her back around. "You have come from a distant realm. For what?"

Once again, Cook, whose name was once—and will be again—Mira, does not know what to say.

Perhaps it was foolish to come here. To the home of the Graces, to the land of Fairendale, to the castle where she is a cook.

"Love is often foolish," says the red-haired Grace. "And yet it is the only thing that can save us."

Cook feels the words blaze into her chest and settle there. Yes. Love is the only thing that has ever saved the world.

"How long have you worn your bear skin?" the brown-skinned Grace says.

"I am recording the time," Cook says.

"Do not wear it for too long," the Grace says. "You know what happens when you do."

Yes. It has been foremost in Cook's mind of late. She has, this time around, worn her bear skin much longer than she has ever worn it before. If a shapeshifter like Cook dons her animal skin for too long, she will be unable to shift back into her human form. No one knows just how long that time is; those who might know have become animals, and not all shape-shifting animals are permitted to talk to humans.

"Perhaps you should remain with us for a day or two," the Grace says. "In your human form."

"There is work to be done," Cook says. "I must find my people."

"There are not many of you who remain," the Grace says.

"There are enough," Cook says. She does not know how she knows this; she simply does. "I will find them. And we will return to you when you call."

"Go, then," the Grace says. "And may you have safe and triumphant travels."

Cook bounds off into the thicker part of the forest, and, once there, she shifts back into her human skin. It is good to know it can still be done. She walks through the forest on two strong legs, summoning a swirl of leaves from the forest floor that becomes a simple brown dress. She enchants another swirl of leaves, and a brown cloak falls upon her shoulders.

She walks all the way to the village of Lincastle, and not a creature disturbs her on her way.

She will eat as a human tonight.

Ruby, one of the lost children of Fairendale, has made for herself a fine, if lopsided, wooden home out of the trees of the forest in which she awoke. She does not have enough expertise in magical studies to make this home invisible, so she is, of course, vulnerable to any who might pass through these woods, but she is well removed from the pathway cutting through the woods, which she noticed on one of her first days of observation. She suspects many have traveled that pathway, but there were no such signs that any traveled in this particular part of the forest. So this is where she built her home.

Her father, who was an assistant to Garron, the head gardener in the village of Fairendale, taught her the ways of survival well, though it was mostly unintended, a study in observation. Ruby knows how to gather the wild herbs of the forest and how to transplant them into a garden of her own. And this she has done with much care and pleasure. In her garden she grows all manner of green herbs and wild roots, the kind that can withstand a bit of chill. The land in which she finds herself is colder than that of Fairendale, but her father also taught Ruby how to use dried-out plants to weave baskets, and, if necessary, scratchy blankets that provide a semblance of warmth. She has a fire in her small, leaning abode, and she uses it faithfully.

Because Ruby knows where to plant things so that they yield the most pickings, how to rotate crops so that the soil does not become tired and weak, and when to properly harvest what she is growing, she has, for many days and nights, fed herself completely from her garden. She must eat more often, perhaps, than she would if she had a hearty side of lamb or a large slab of lamb's butter, but she is not hungry, even if she is not quite full. She has even ventured into a bit of experimental cooking, roasting roots over the fire in the corner of her wooden house. She always watches this fire carefully to ensure it does not burn down the whole structure. Her father taught her, among his many other lessons, to be solemnly careful with fire.

During the day she watches the birds. She does not fear the creatures of the forest, for her father never found it necessary to tell her much about them. He always knew that his daughter was a wise girl, capable of doing the right thing, approaching circumstances with courage, and choosing kindness always. (If you might permit me a short digression, I must also point out that there was another reason Ruby's father did not teach her about the creatures of the forest. By nature, her father is a skeptical man. He does not entirely believe the stories about the creatures of the woods that are told to every other child in Fairendale. So he chose to simply ignore them.)

So it is that Ruby is blissfully unaware of the creatures that might very well be eyeing her, even now, and thinking what a fine meal she would make.

Ruby is, for the most part, satisfied with her life in the woods.

Sometimes, however, she feels a bit lonely. She longs for some human interaction. She always enjoyed attending the magic lessons with the girls of Fairendale village, offered in the small and cozy home of Arthur and Maude, not only because it excused her from weeding the gardens with her father—he would make her do it later anyway, so it was not exactly a permanent respite—but also because it provided an opportunity to connect with others. She misses the friendships she had back in Fairendale. She wonders about the other girls. Have they managed on their own? Will she ever see them again?

She occasionally tries to distract herself from these thoughts by talking to the limbs around her. "Good day," she will say, and then she will giggle. It is silly to talk to trees. They cannot hear you.

Today the trees bend and sway, and a whisper hovers near her right ear. Ruby tilts her head. *Go into the village,* the whisper says. She looks around.

"Who is there?" she says, but, of course, there is no one.

Two more times the whisper meets her ear, and, startled, she looks up, to the side, behind, and back up. Two more times she sees no one.

She cannot go into the village. This is not Fairendale —of that she can be sure (she often stole into the woods outside Fairendale, and they looked nothing like these; she has deduced that they are not the same woods). She is unsure, however, what sorts of dangers might await her in this village, though danger, her father used to tell her, lives everywhere. By rising in the morning one courts danger, and one must always decide, at one point or another, whether danger is enough to still action or embolden it.

Her father had always encouraged her to allow danger to embolden her action. But still Ruby hesitates.

Still she steps around her garden, plucking what plants are ready for harvesting. She lays the bounty carefully in her woven basket.

And then, one more time, the whisper reaches her ears. *Go into the village*, it says. And this time she sets down her basket on the ground in front of her leaning home and searches for the well-worn path she is sure leads toward whatever village to which she has come, by way of a Vanishing spell.

She does not take her magical staff or the small dagger her father gave her on her twelfth birthday. She is almost to the village, none of which she can see because of the large stone walls that hide it, before she realizes that she has left these necessary tools behind.

But she does not turn around. Perhaps they will not be so necessary today. After all, the village is protected by a fortress.

She remembers this village from her studies: Rosehaven. It is supposed to have the most beautiful white roses in the realm.

Ruby smiles.

Questions

Vivian was the lucky girl who married King Sebastien, the ruler of Fairendale, the most powerful land in the realm. She did not know him all that well, but she found him very handsome. When she was led into the royal throne room, along with a host of other beautiful women, and paraded before the throne of the new king, she was commanded to demonstrate the extent of her magical gift, which she did quite readily. She was not able to practice it much in the kingdom of Eastermoor, where she lived, at least not out in the open—she had her ways, of course—but hers was such a powerful gift, still, that her shadow engulfed all the others.

She had only just warmed up, too. She had turned a bird into a living object—a quill that wrote all by itself, which she thought was brilliant—and no sooner had she done this when the handsome king smiled at her and said, "I will take that one."

It was an impersonal introduction, but Vivian did not let it bother her. She knew, eventually, that she would win the king's heart and not just his admiration.

In the days after, the castle attendants dressed her in beautiful blue-green gowns that so matched her eyes they practically glowed. Her maidservant was adept at twisting Vivian's red locks into a crown of its own on her head. She had seen the king staring at her a time or two, and this made her smile. Once, she even saw his hand reach out as though to touch her beautiful hair, and then he looked away at his manservant, an old, bent, gray man. This man was gray everywhere. He was gray on top and gray on his skin and gray on every piece of clothing he chose to wear. Vivian thought he was quite dull and would have liked to splash a bit of color on his robe.

After her marriage to the king, Queen Vivian (she giggled at the title) felt compelled to open up the windows of Fairendale castle and let the light through. She loved the light, and the castle was very dark. She thought its halls and melancholy rooms could be improved greatly with a bit of light. She appointed a Torch Lighter, who would, every day, set ablaze all the torches down the dark hallways and passages of the castle (there were many). It took an entire day to light them all. Fortunately, she helped out with the nightly extinguishing by doing a bit of simple magic.

King Sebastien left Queen Vivian to her own devices most of the time. She was only a girl of fifteen when they married, so she was very much intrigued by the twists and turns of the large castle. She explored them every day and nearly always stumbled upon a new room or passage that she had not discovered before. It was as though the castle in this land was magical as well. It was enchanting and amused her for days and months on end. There were sitting rooms that had not been used in centuries, judging by their outdated furnishings. There were bedrooms for guests with silky golden coverlets and royal blue coverlets and fiery scarlet coverlets; the doors to these bedrooms remained closed, but they were cleaned and prepared regularly, always awaiting occupants. There were masterpieces painted onto ceilings and along the passages of hallways. Vivian could spend whole days staring at the brush strokes that had made them.

But her favorite place, by far, was the castle library.

Shelves that reached all the way up to the ceiling, which was quite far, were filled with ancient texts with golden script on their bindings. They were all different sizes of thickness and height, and they called to Queen Vivian most every morning. She would curl up in a small blue cushioned chair, beside the fire that one of the servants would stoke every morning, knowing she would not be long in arriving. She would read for hours upon hours, until the urge to move thrust her from the chair and sent her dancing down the hallways once more.

If there were one word to describe Queen Vivian, it would be: splendor. She was splendor itself. Magnificent in her gift, shining in her beauty, insatiable in her wonder and curiosity. She brought light and joy to the castle of Fairendale, even under the iron rule of King Sebastien.

Queen Vivian lavished attention upon her servants. She had no qualms about telling them how glad she was to be there, that she hoped their stay was wonderful, that she wondered if they had anything they needed. The servants seemed surprised by their queen's attentions, but Queen Vivian had been the daughter of a working woman. She knew that the servants worked exceedingly hard so that she could have extravagant comforts, because she had seen her mother do the same.

And because of this attention, the servants had no trouble lavishing attention on their queen. The castle seamstress, when not engaged with dresses or a new robe for the king, used her time to sew Queen Vivian a cover for her bed that was, perhaps, the grandest the kingdom had ever seen. The blue-green fabric from which it was made shimmered and shifted color before the queen's eyes. She clapped her hands in wonder when she saw it. The castle painter, when not occupied with a new wall on which to paint or an old wall to be restored, crafted on the queen's bedroom wall, facing north, a picture of the glittering snow of White Wind, a land the queen had never seen. She laughed merrily when she saw it. The castle manager, when not too busy organizing receptions for visiting dignitaries or planning the day's menu, would send for the village bookbinder and commission a new book for the queen. Queen Vivian hugged the castle manager every time a new book arrived and then raced off to the library to consume it as quickly as she might.

When Queen Vivian's steps sounded in the mornings, all the castle staff stood a bit straighter and smiled a bit brighter.

Even the king's men enjoyed talking with her, though she tried not to join their banter very often; she had once seen a dark look on King Sebastien's face when she had burst out laughing at something his captain had said. She knew he was jealous, and the thought made her very happy.

What Queen Vivian had never told anyone, and what

she would never tell, is that her magic was of a different sort than the kind most sorceresses had. Her magic could sway minds. She could heal the emotions of others. She could bend them, if she wished. She had discovered this when she was quite young, on a day when her mother was in the middle of scolding her for something foolish she had done—she could not even remember what— and, in the middle of the scolding, when Vivian's hand reached, almost instinctually, for her staff, her mother's face softened, and she opened her arms to her daughter.

Queen Vivian used this gift on her husband. In time, he came to look on her as something more than a silly child. He could see the way that she brightened the castle and made it much lovelier, because she coaxed him into it, gently, invisibly, persistently.

The king, when Queen Vivian first came to the castle, did not hold a very high opinion of women. They were expendable, had nothing important to say, served as beautiful decorations. She supposed this was why he did not let her sit in on throne room meetings or even diplomatic dinners. But Queen Vivian studied in the castle library and began to know all there was to know about government and politics and the history of the land. She overheard King Sebastien rage about how the kingdoms were still angry with him, though the Great

Battle had taken place twenty-three years ago. She could sense fear in his raging. He was afraid that the other lands would bring war. He lived in fear of it, in fact.

When King Sebastien brought Queen Vivian into a meeting that was not so much a meeting as it was simply a fine dinner, she would only smile demurely and dip her head, as though she had nothing to say. But her power worked relentlessly on the king during those dinners. He would end them in very good humor and with unexpected kindnesses toward the dignitaries present, who came from the neighboring lands around Fairendale.

Those political visits began to dwindle, however, and Queen Vivian suspected that her magic was not allowed application frequently enough.

One day King Sebastien stopped Queen Vivian on her way down a long hallway that had just been lit with torches. The light shifted and flashed against the king's face. "Why do you light all these torches?" he said, gesturing around. His robe was green today, fringed with shimmery silver.

She smiled at him and dipped her head. "I enjoy the light," she said. "And Bran likes to feel useful." She was speaking of the man who lit torches.

The king's smile vanished, and he stalked away without another word.

Another day, she was in the castle gardens, which she loved to visit, not only for the flowers but for the beautiful, bright vegetables that grew in abundance. She touched her staff to the ground and made the garden practically overflow. Her heart felt happy seeing so much life, which could then be passed along to the people of her village. She did not know, then, that all the surplus bounty would go only on the shelves of the castle kitchen, where it would remain until it rotted. It would not benefit the people at all; the king did not believe in feeding his people. She had no idea.

King Sebastien's voice behind her startled her. "Why do you make the garden overflow with vegetables?" he said.

"Because I love to feed my people," Queen Vivian said.

The king's face, this time, grew very dark, but still he said nothing. He looked to be thinking, and she gripped her staff and allowed him to think but shaped those thoughts, just a little, for him. She smiled at him, and she could almost see the ghost of a smile looking back at her. He turned and walked away.

Another day, she was talking with the captain of the king's guard, who was a graying, wrinkled man. She was telling him about her land of Eastermoor and how the people there believed in freedom, mostly. And caring for the land, but caring for it in its own way. Children could run in fields and inside the woods and do whatever they wished. She had done that as a child.

"Did you like it in that land, with so much freedom?" King Sebastien said, joining the two.

"Oh, yes," Queen Vivian said. "Very much so."

"You have much freedom here as well," King Sebastien said.

"Yes," Queen Vivian said. "Though it is a lonely sort of freedom."

The king looked at her, and she cast her eyes to the ground.

"You know the names of all the people here," he said.

"I do, Your Grace," she said. "It is kind to call a person by his name."

"And what do you call me?" he said.

Queen Vivian looked up. She smiled at him fully. "I call you Husband," she said.

And this time, the king smiled, too.

The king's face softened considerably in the days and years after he married Queen Vivian. Her magic worked the most wonders of all on him.

Possibilities

There is a scuttling sound in the corner of the dungeons beneath the dungeons of Fairendale castle, and while the blind girl who is trapped in this prison, along with many other children, has heard many sounds similar to it in the last several days, this time the sound crinkles and folds at the corners, rendering it the slightest bit different. It is one that can be heard by every person who lies or sits or pretends to sleep in an iron cell.

They gasp.

It is, perhaps, even more frightening that the sound happens in complete and utter darkness. Imagine, if you will, the darkest place you could possibly be, and then introduce into that place a *click-scratch, click-scratch, click-scratch* sound. The children huddle closer to one another. Some of them even wrap their arms around their neighbor, though it is impossible to tell whose arms belong to whom.

Yerin is the only prophet in this place who remains awake. He is the only one who lifts himself and says, "What is it?" which, alas, does not assuage the fears of the children at all. It only escalates them. Some in this dungeon are predisposed to think the worst. They believe that the prophets who have been piled at the back of their cell—sleeping or decomposing, no one knows— have risen again. And it is true that this is possible in a land such as this one, but I am happy to report that the scratching belongs to some other explanation.

Yerin shuffles forward on his rump. He pulls himself to his knees, gripping the iron bars of the cell, trying to still his hands from their shaking. His dreams have been fraught with dark and terrible things, and, having just been woken by the unfamiliar sound piercing the silence of the dungeons, the cloud of fear stretches, shifts, and plants itself in the middle of his chest.

The scratching comes closer—footsteps, it sounds like. But footsteps belonging to no man.

"Who goes there?" Yerin calls out into the blackness.

No one answers. There is more scratching, more footsteps, more silence. It is a rhythm: *click, scratch, silence. Click, scratch, silence.* Something clatters. Something else thuds against the floor. Yerin looks toward the neighboring cell, his eyes roaming everywhere, but no matter where he looks, he can detect no blue glow. Complete and utter darkness is better than a blue glow when that blue glow has, in the past, belonged to a pile of bones.

Still, the fear cuts off his breath. He can no longer breathe or speak.

"Show yourself," says the girl, Agnes, who has pulled herself up beside him. She cannot see, for she is blind, but her courage is contagious, and Yerin grunts in response.

"Who is there?" he says.

They listen. There is nothing.

"Perhaps it was only the castle shifting," Yerin says, and as the words climb out, they ring hollow and untrue.

Yerin and Agnes remain at the bars. The dungeons remain silent. And when they are about to let go of the bars, the sound amplifies, multiplies, and suddenly there is not only one *click-scratch*, there are several. A child releases a piercing scream. One bubbles up in Yerin's mouth, but he presses his hand to his lips and wills it to remain inside. He cannot frighten the children. But a very small white shape gathers in the corner of the dungeons, near the stairs Calvin, the boy who feeds them, descends when he is able to visit. A stomach rumbles behind Yerin. A child begins to cry. The white shape moves closer in jerking motions, as though running and stopping and running and stopping and running again. Yerin watches with a horror that cannot be contained. It inches out his mouth in a moan.

But then the shape stops. Another scratch sounds, and an explosion of light appears. It is so bright that everyone in the cell must turn away, with an arm in front of their eyes. They utter a collective yell of surprise.

A small voice reaches out from the dark. "Well," it says. "This place is already inhabited."

"There are many in here," says another voice, squeakier than the first.

A third voice grunts.

"But still room enough for us," the first voice says. "We are small."

Yerin blinks in the blinding light. He blinks again and again. And finally his eyes have adjusted. A match burns in the hand of a mouse. A mouse wearing dark black glasses that shield his eyes from view. A mouse walking on two feet. A mouse carrying what looks like a miniature staff.

A match in the hand of a mouse? A mouse wearing dark black glasses? A mouse walking on two feet? A mouse carrying a staff?

Yerin shakes his head. He must be locked in a strange dream.

"Hello," the mouse says.

No one speaks. All are much too terrified to even try.

"I know you are there," the mouse says. He is the largest one, round and fat. The match flickers and burns out. "Light me another, Timmy," he says.

"Straight away, Gus," says another, and the light returns, shaky for a moment but then blazing.

"Now then," says the first mouse, the one called Gus. "I cannot see you. But I can smell you. I know you are here."

Yerin glances toward the bones. There they are, still crumpled in the corner of the adjacent cell. He glances back at the bodies of the prophets. They, too, remain, still piled in the back of this largest cell in the dungeon.

"It smells something awful in here," says Timmy.

"Like dead ones," says Gus. "But there are living ones, too."

The light flickers out.

"I suppose we do not need light if we are the only ones here." Yerin thinks it is Gus who says the words.

The darkness, so large and complete, rouses Yerin. "What do you want?" he says, at last locating his words and the courage to speak them.

"See?" Gus says. "I knew they were not all dead." The match blazes and immediately flickers out. "We will have to find something more permanent," he says. "Light me another, Timmy."

"Right away, Gus," Timmy says, and another match sparks to life. It towers comically over the small mouse.

"You do not have to be afraid of us," Gus says. He walks—on two feet!—a bit closer to the iron bars. The children, unaware that they are even doing it, back away. But Yerin and Agnes remain at the bars. "I can smell your fear, but I assure you that we are friendly mice. Florence can be a bit grumpy sometimes."

At this, the third mouse, taller and wider than the other two, growls a tiny mouse growl. The children nearly laugh, though at the last moment, they keep their wits about them. They have never encountered an angry mouse, and they do not want to encounter one today.

When you have lived so long in the dark, everything seems dangerous.

"We will not bother you," Gus says. "We only need somewhere to sleep now and then, somewhere the people of the castle will not think to look. Kitchens are too obvious."

"There are other dungeons," Yerin says. "Why

these?"

Gus considers this for a moment. He tilts his head this way and that way. But no answer seems to be good enough for him, so he simply says, "I cannot remember. I know there was a reason."

"Who is it?" Agnes says.

Yerin remembers then that she cannot see the figures before them. "Three mice," he says. "Blind ones. Who walk." He knows how outrageously mad this sounds. But he is seeing it with his own two eyes.

"Oh," Agnes says. It is clear by the wide smile on her face that she is delighted by this turn of events, though Agnes is a child who is delighted by most things in life. It is one of the attributes her father, Sir Merrick, second in command to Captain Sir Greyson of the King's Guard in Fairendale, loved most about her. He always said she could turn the grayest day into one beaming with sunshine. "I did not know that mice could talk to people."

Gus shoves his dark glasses up his tiny black nose. "Of course mice can talk," he says. "At least, *we* can talk." He seems to consider this for a moment, too. "Though, come to think of it, I have never met another mouse who could talk to a human." While he is speaking, the match's flame climbs closer to his fingers. The children watch, mesmerized, as fire eats wood. Will it also eat the tiny hand of a mouse? But just when the fire is about to overtake him, Florence moves so quickly they hardly see her, and the flame extinguishes, sending them back into immediate and pervasive darkness, until the whole routine begins again.

"Where were we?" Gus says.

"You are a talking mouse," Agnes says.

"Are you sure I am a mouse?" Gus says.

"Well, I cannot see you," Agnes says. "I am blind as well. But Yerin says you are a mouse."

"And we can trust Yerin?" Gus says.

"Yerin is the wisest man there is, besides my father," Agnes says. A shade of sadness lingers on the last of her words.

Yerin searches his mind for something that calls to him. There was a story once, was there not? About three blind mice? Two men and a woman who had been turned into rodents? Alas, it was long ago when he read a story like that one, and he does not remember the details. But because he has never before met an animal that could talk so capably with people, as these three blind mice do, he allows himself to believe that they are, at their essence, human, rather than rodent. This, perhaps, makes it easier for him to swallow that he is talking to a mouse. Three of them. Who walk on their two hind feet and wear dark glasses that conceal their eyes and carry miniature staffs. He shakes his head.

"Well, then, I suppose we can trust the wisest man there is," Gus says.

"Have you lived at the castle long?" Yerin says. "We have never seen you here."

"We have only just arrived," Gus says. "We have traveled a long distance, though I cannot remember why."

A small knot of hope unfolds in Yerin's heart.

"Have you lived long at the castle?" Gus says.

"For ever so long," Agnes says.

"But this is a dungeon," Gus says. "What have you done wrong?"

"We are alive," Agnes says. "That is the only thing we have ever done wrong." The words hang in the air like a heavy cloud. "The king of this land put us here. He is searching for a magical boy."

"And is the magical boy here?" Gus says.

"No," Agnes says.

"Then why do you remain?" Gus says.

"Because the king has forgotten who he is," Yerin says. "The king has allowed the power of a throne to twist his mind and heart. So we remain."

The mice are silent for a time, and then they talk

amongst themselves as if they are the only ones in the dungeons.

"The woman said something about children, did she not?" Gus says.

"She certainly did," Timmy says. "I simply cannot remember exactly what it was."

Florence grunts.

Gus taps his tiny head with one finger. "She said find a boy," he says. "That is all."

"Find a boy," Timmy says. "Why, that could mean anything."

A boy. Yerin knows who the boy is. He cries out, and the mice turn in his direction.

"You search for a boy," Yerin says.

"A boy in this castle," Gus says. "A boy who can help. Am I correct in remembering this?"

"Yes," Timmy says.

Florence grunts.

"I know a boy in the castle who can help," Yerin says.

"Yes, Calvin!" Agnes says. Yerin places his hand on her arm.

"There is a boy who searches for a key," Yerin says. "Did your master tell you anything about a key?"

"Master?" Gus says. "We have no master."

"You spoke of a woman," Yerin says.

"She is not our master," Gus says. "She is only a woman who sent us into the woods."

"So you have been in the woods," Yerin says.

"It is the only way to get to Fairendale from Lincastle," Gus says. "We traveled many days and many nights, and now we are here. And I have forgotten why."

"There is a boy who searches for a key," Yerin says. "Perhaps you know where it is."

"I know nothing of a key," Gus says. The other two mice nod. "I only know of a boy. Where is the boy? Is he in here with you?"

"No," Yerin says. "He is a servant of the castle."

"A servant of the castle," Gus says. "Yes, that sounds like a boy who can help us, as she said."

"Who said?" Yerin says.

"The woman," Gus says.

"What does this woman look like? Where did you meet her? Is she old, with ebony skin and threads of braided hair that twist like snakes?" Yerin cannot stop the words now, hope flying from his lips.

"We are blind," Gus says. "We have never seen her. Her voice is very beautiful, and I imagine she is, too."

"There was another question," Timmy says.

"What was it again?" Gus says.

"Where did you meet her," Timmy says.

"Ah, yes," Gus says. "I do not know. We have always known her. She lives in Lincastle, and the people in the village call her the Evil Queen. I do not know her name."

Yerin steps back from the bars, sorrow blasting into his shoulders. He had hoped, for a moment, that the woman from whom they came was Aleen. He hopes, still, that she is not dead, only missing, though he knows full well the consequences of a prophet's One Last Great Act, when they are permitted one last act of magic on the day of their one hundred forty-third birthday. A prophet who uses his One Last Great Act dies. And Aleen used hers.

As quickly as the sorrow arrives, Yerin thrusts it away. The Evil Queen. He has heard of the Evil Queen—great and terrible things about her, in fact. He cannot say whether she is on their side or the side of another. Should he protect the boy from the mice, then, or should he consider them allies?

It is all too confusing, too sudden, too overwhelming. Yerin lets out a long breath.

"Well, then," Gus says. "Are we permitted to stay here for a time?"

No one says anything. Yerin is too tired. He only nods. Another match has come and gone, and one is lit in its place. No one sees Yerin's nod, for it happened at the exact moment the match expired. The girl, Agnes, presses her cheeks against the iron bars.

"We would be glad to have you," she says. "And you can do something for us, if you wish. It would be most helpful."

"And what is that?" Gus says, in the most accommodating voice one has ever heard from a rodent.

"You can bring us information," Agnes says. "Tell us what goes on in the castle and the village. Perhaps it will help us with our own plans."

Yerin's gaze moves to the girl. Plans? They do not have plans. But he sees, by the buoyant tilt of her chin, that he is wrong. She has a great many plans. She has simply not shared them.

A surprised sound escapes his lips. "Oh," he says. "Oh," he says again, and this time it is an exclamation of pleasure.

Community, you see, is a beautiful thing—even one that is forged in a dungeon. When one member of a community, Yerin in this instance, loses hope and faith and strength, another member of the community, Agnes, can step into the gap and close it. It is quite extraordinary.

"And perhaps you might bring us some food?" says a small boy, no more than eight years old, from the back of the group. He shuffles forward, a limp hitching his walk.

"I believe that could be arranged," Gus says.

"Yes," Timmy says. "We will need food. May as well share it."

Florence lets out what sounds like another mouse grunt.

"There is a boy who brings us food," Yerin says. "It is not enough, but we will share ours as well." He points toward the ceiling, to the right of where he stands, forgetting momentarily that he is speaking to three blind mice. "Water drips through a weak spot in the ceiling. It has kept us alive all these days."

"Do not worry about food," Gus says. "Mice are very good at gathering and transporting."

"Very good," Timmy says.

Florence grunts.

"And what might we give you in return?" Yerin says.

"Company," Gus says. "That is all we need." He tilts his head again, his nose sniffing the air.

"Do you know any stories?" Agnes says.

"We know many stories," Gus says. "We know happy ones and sad ones and terrifying ones and adventuresome ones. We keep a large collection of redemption stories in our small brains. You would be surprised to know how many. What kind would you like to hear?"

"What is a redemption story?" says the small boy.

"It is the only story that has ever been told," Gus says. "Every story since the beginning of time is a redemption story."

"I would like to hear one of those," the small boy says.

"And I know just the one," Gus says.

The children settle in. The mouse begins, weaving a story's threads in a net around the children, a net that guards and protects and changes, in the smallest little way. It is the best kind of story, and even Yerin smiles at this telling, hope tiptoeing back into his heart.

The Enchantress and the Huntsman sit around a fire, as they always do on their travels. Their days have grown quite predictable on their quest to gather all the lost children of Fairendale for King Willis, who demanded the children's capture after it was discovered that a magical boy lived in Fairendale, under the cover of a secret.

Rise with the sun, eat around a fire, travel for most of the day, eat again around a fire, and retire for the night. This is the way their days have proceeded for many days now. Rise, eat, travel, eat, retire. Rise, eat, travel, eat, retire. The Enchantress has never much liked routine and predictability, but she is confounded as to how she might shake up their days a bit. She certainly would not like to introduce danger into the equation. The Huntsman has already survived the magic jabbed into him when he walked through a fairy ring, as well as the poison from a serpent in the Were Woods of Eastermoor, or very near it.

"Where is it we travel next?" the Huntsman says.

The Enchantress clears her throat. She has not yet wanted to tell him, for they are backtracking with this latest child revealed by her magical looking ball. She can only go where the looking ball tells her to go, and, unfortunately, it only shows one child at a time. So even though they have already captured a child from the land of Rosehaven, they must now return to capture another.

She stalls. "We will find one of the lost girls," she says. "This one has become an old crone. An old magical crone."

"But where is she?" the Huntsman says.

"Rosehaven," the Enchantress says, wincing slightly at the word but lifting it at the end so that it seems light and cheerful. She adds a smile, but it is tight, fabricated, wrong.

She feels the Huntsman's eyes move to her, but she

does not meet them. And perhaps because she does not meet them, he says, "Rosehaven? Have we not already been to this land?"

"Yes," she says. She lifts her chin. "You know that I can only go where the ball tells me to go." She meets his eyes now, and the fire flickers within his. He is challenging her, but she is unsure of what he asks.

"You do not think this is some dangerous game?" he says at last. "Where did this ball come from in the first place?"

She does not know if she should tell him this. But the doubts, of late, have been quite loud in her mind. And they are also quite heavy. She could use a bit of assistance carrying them. So she says, "I lived in the Weeping Woods. I did not always live in the Weeping Woods, but when I became an Enchantress, the woods drew me there somehow."

"I thought you did not believe in fate," the Huntsman says.

"I cannot explain what drew me," the Enchantress says. She clenches her teeth. "I only know that when I arrived, there was a house waiting for me. And this ball was inside it."

The Huntsman stares at her, as though he expects her to say that it did not happen in this way at all, that she is only telling an elaborate story. But it is the truth. And she feels the doubt grow heavier on her shoulders.

"And you did not question to whom this house or this ball belonged?" the Huntsman says.

"It belonged to me," the Enchantress says. "It is the only explanation."

"It is not the only explanation," the Huntsman says, and she can tell, by the pitch of his voice, that he is angry now. "Do you not know that these woods twisting through all the lands are full of dark magic? Creatures for which we do not even have names? Sorcery that cannot be explained?"

"Of course I do," she says, and now her voice has risen. It rings out into the night sky, carrying with it her fear and uncertainty and, yes, even her loneliness.

It is a difficult, lonely thing being an Enchantress.

The Huntsman does not speak for some time. The Enchantress stares at her hands, thoughts flipping through her mind. *Suppose it is a trick. Suppose someone else controls the ball. Suppose the house and the ball were not mine to find.*

When the Huntsman finally speaks, the Enchantress wishes he had remained silent. "If someone else controls the ball..." he says. "If someone else leads us astray..." He does not finish.

The Enchantress feels a pebble lodge in the back of her throat. "I can only hope." They are the only words she can manage before her voice breaks in two.

The Huntsman moves closer to her. "Well, if it is a game," he says, "then we shall play it better."

The Enchantress raises her eyes to his and sees that he is genuine, earnest, perfectly confident that they will do just that. She dips her head, a burn prickling her nose. She says nothing. She feels more than sees the Huntsman shiver. She lifts her eyes. He has been wearing the colorful blanket that she provided him several nights past, like a coat of many colors. "The blanket is not warm enough," she says. "We must make you a fur cape."

"It is nothing," the Huntsman says.

"Rosehaven is, at least, warmer than White Wind," the Enchantress says. The Huntsman smiles. Her face warms in his amusement.

After a time, the Huntsman says, "Do you know all the children's names?" She is so startled by the question that she nearly gasps. His eyes seem to sink all the way into her, reading her secrets.

Yes. She knows the name of every lost twelve-year-old. But she cannot tell him this. It would only raise more questions. So she says, "Do you?"

He does not answer her either. He stares at the

flames. "Sometimes I wonder if these children will be forgotten," he says. "If their names will never mean anything to the kingdom of Fairendale. They are only numbers to the king."

The Enchantress stares at the flames as well. She does not know what she can say, if there is, in fact, anything she can say.

Behind them, one of the blackbirds twitters. They both turn to look at the birds imprisoned in their iron cages.

"Do you think they will remember living as blackbirds?" the Huntsman says.

"I do not know," the Enchantress says. What she does not say is that she also does not know if she can transform them from blackbirds back to children. It is not a conversation she would like to have right now.

"I hope they do not," he says. "No child should be imprisoned behind a cage."

The Enchantress rises, feeling a warmth in her cheeks and neck that drive her from the heat of the fire. "It is time for rest," she says. "We shall move on at first light."

"Back to Rosehaven," the Huntsman says, his face glowing in the fire. His eyebrows draw low over his eyes. He wears his thinking face.

"See that the horse is adequately watered before we

depart," the Enchantress says. The Huntsman does not answer.

She leaves him to stare into the flames and make sense of what he can.

The first person Ruby spies in the village of Rosehaven is a girl with the most beautiful hair she has ever seen. The girl's hair is a glistening gold, tied up in so many large knots that it appears to occasionally make her head tilt to one side or the other. Judging by the tensed muscles in the girl's neck, the hair must be very heavy and very long, for what is not tied in bulky knots still reaches the ground and fans out on the cobblestone path around the village fountains, where the girl sits and talks to a small girl clothed in a tattered brown dress.

Ruby tilts her own head to the side. What would possess a girl to grow her hair so long? And by what magic? Ruby has been alive twelve years, and she has only cut her hair once. Still it only reaches the middle of her back. The girl does not appear all that much older than Ruby.

A woman dressed in shimmering blue and wearing the same golden hair, though not nearly so long, lays a hand on the girl's shoulder. The girl looks up and is momentarily thrown off balance by her hair. She rights herself and stands. A man approaches and takes her other arm. He has a black mustache that twirls up at the ends of it in two neatly formed spirals. Black hair rises in random shocks around his head, as though he had an unfortunate encounter with a stunning machine, which Ruby once heard the boys of Fairendale discussing on their way through the village streets. It is an ancient machine used in torture, but it appears that this man uses one to comb his hair.

The thought makes Ruby giggle.

"I am all out of chamomile," Ruby hears the girl say.

Ruby's heart quickens. She has chamomile in her garden. It is a fragile flower, and it does not grow well in cold temperatures, but she has managed to do it. She has applied a bit of magic. Chamomile is good for soothing nerves and summoning sleep. Perhaps if she could offer her stock, she might make a friend.

"And chamomile is how you keep your face beautiful, no?" the man says, touching the girl's smooth cheek.

"Yes, Father," the girl says. She glances at the people breezing past them.

Ruby feels a familiar ache in her chest. How she misses her father. She did not even have a chance to say goodbye.

"And the apothecary does not have any?" the woman says.

"No, Mother," the girl says.

"Well, Rapunzel," her father says. "I am sure we can locate some chamomile somewhere." His voice is jolly and amused, but Rapunzel appears quite worried.

Ruby wonders how the girl uses the herb to beautify her face. She has never heard of such a thing. Does Rapunzel wear it as a paste? Or does she drink it as a tea? Ruby has only known chamomile for its calming effects. She would use it often to calm down her father when news from the castle arrived at the village and did not sit well with him—which was nearly every time news arrived. Her father was a greatly outspoken man. She always admired that about him, but she found it necessary to calm his passionate diatribes now and again by slipping a bit of chamomile into his tea.

"I cannot properly perform my beauty routine without the herb," Rapunzel says.

Her father's face falls a bit, and he looks perplexed, as though he does not know what to say. Rapunzel's mother pats the girl's hand. "Well, then, perhaps we might send for it from another land," she says. "I am sure someone has some chamomile."

Ruby nearly steps forward then to offer her own supply of the herb. But something holds her back. What if they can tell, upon looking at her, that she is one of the lost children of Fairendale? What if they sent her back?

And would that be so bad?

When she considers reuniting with her father, no. But when she considers the fate of all magical children, as declared by the king of Fairendale, then yes, very much so.

Now she is quite ready to run, to escape this unknown village and its unknown people. But, again, something holds her back.

A tear drops from Rapunzel's large, pale blue eye. "But what will happen if my beauty fades?" she says.

"The prince will love you even without your lovely face," her mother says.

"There are many other girls in this village," Rapunzel says. "He will be advised to cast me away for another."

"He will not do it," her father says, and he puffs himself up, granting a bit of importance to his stature. "We have made a binding agreement. And he is an honorable boy."

"But the agreement was made for the most beautiful girl in the land," Rapunzel says, her voice softer now. "I will not be the most beautiful girl in the land without chamomile to preserve and smooth my face."

"Nonsense," her mother says. They are speaking in whispers, and somehow Ruby can hear them. She marvels at this. "There is more to beauty than a face. You have your heart. That has always been beautiful, and no herb will ever take that away or strengthen it. And the prince, I believe, knows this."

"But the king desires the most beautiful girl for Prince Cole," Rapunzel says. "He will never see me among the rest. And then you…"

"Do not worry about us," her father says. He pats her arm, and then he wraps her in a tight embrace that wraps around Ruby, too. He pulls away but keeps his hands on her arms. "Listen to me. It is not your responsibility to care for your father and your mother. It is our responsibility to care for you."

"But my marriage to the prince is the only thing that will erase your debt," Rapunzel says.

"We will manage in other ways," her mother says. She glances around, as though looking to ensure that no one in the village has heard their exchange of words. Her eyes move over Ruby, who glances away, and on to some men outside a tavern and then back to her daughter. "Perhaps we should continue our discussion at home."

"I am meeting the prince," Rapunzel says. Her

parents nod, kiss their daughter's cheek, and walk away from the fountain.

Ruby watches Rapunzel wait, assesses the feeling in her gut—as her father always taught her to do—and then, feeling no trace of alarm, approaches Rapunzel.

"Hello," she says. "I know where you might find some chamomile."

Rapunzel looks up at her and then down at the ground. "Chamomile?" she says. "Why would I need chamomile?"

"I overheard you," Ruby says, lowering her voice. "But your secret is safe." She tries to arrange her face into the most accommodating expression she can manage. She does not know if she succeeds. So she says, "I grow chamomile in my garden."

Rapunzel looks at her again, and this time her eyes hold questions. "But there is no one in Rosehaven who can grow chamomile." Her eyes narrow. "It is much too cold here. Is this some kind of trick?"

"No," Ruby says. "I live in the woods. My father taught me how to grow herbs in all sorts of climates— warm or cold." She hopes the girl will believe her.

Rapunzel stares at her for what seems like a very long time. Her eyes narrow. "I have never seen you in this village."

Ruby glances away. "There are many people in this village," she says.

"But you have come from somewhere else," Rapunzel says. "You have a different look than even the poor of this village."

Ruby does not answer. She simply says. "I would like to gift you with some chamomile. For your lovely face."

Rapunzel shakes her head, and it lolls a bit to the left. She straightens it. "It is not for my face," she says, and her cheeks turn a curious shade of red.

"Then why do you need it?" Ruby says.

Rapunzel's ice-blue eyes lock on her face. "You are an old woman," she says. "I do not think you would understand."

"Old woman?" Ruby says. She does not feel like an old woman. She is a twelve-year-old girl, or she *was* the last time she checked. She moves to peer into the water of the fountain, and, sure enough, an old woman's face looks back at her. She touches it, marveling at the wrinkles. She has never seen so many wrinkles. Her brown braids are gone as well. They are white now, hanging down her back, tied with a bit of blue string, as they were before. Ruby takes a step back and smiles.

"Well, now that is a surprise." Rapunzel tilts her head—a bit farther than a normal person would because of all that hair. Ruby continues. "Perhaps I need a bit of chamomile, too."

Rapunzel presses her hand to her mouth, but Ruby sees the smile the golden-haired girl tries to suppress. "Where is your home?" Rapunzel says when she has composed herself.

"Not far," Ruby says. "I would be glad to take you."

"Take her where?" says a voice behind them. Rapunzel turns, her eyes brightening instantly. Ruby turns to see a tall boy with piercing blue eyes and sandy hair that flips out from his face as though windblown from running. He wears an orange robe of royalty, beneath which she can see a clean white tunic, smooth black pants, and boots without a hint of a hole in them. He does not wear a crown.

"Prince Cole," Rapunzel says. She curtsies deeply, and Ruby does the same, oblivious to how odd it looks to see an old woman curtsy so effortlessly. Prince Cole is staring at her when she rises.

"I have not seen you around, old woman," he says.

"I am not so very old," Ruby says. Fear makes it difficult to swallow. She has never trusted princes.

But Prince Cole smiles, and Ruby knows, then, that he is not an unkind prince. She smiles widely back at him, unaware that she is missing three front teeth. "And where might you be taking my…" Prince Cole's gaze shifts from Rapunzel to the ground and back to Ruby's face. "My friend?" Ruby sees that he very much loves Rapunzel. Her heart warms.

"To my garden," she says. "She has need of some chamomile."

"Very well," Prince Cole says. "I will join you." He grins at Rapunzel, who grins back, nodding, and then they both turn expectantly to Ruby. She realizes his statement was some sort of question.

"This way," she says, and she begins the walk back into the woods and all the way to her home. Prince Cole and Rapunzel exclaim over her garden as soon as they arrive.

"However did you manage to grow a garden like this?" Prince Cole says. "Is it not much too cold for these herbs?"

"Yes, perhaps," Ruby says. She pulls her staff, a thing that looks almost as old as she has become, from where it leans against the lopsided home. "But I have assistance."

Rapunzel's eyes grow wide. Prince Cole moves in front of her, as though protecting her from what he fears will come. "You are a sorceress," he says, suspicion coiling at the edges of his voice.

"Yes," Ruby says. "But I do not want to harm you. I

am a good sorceress. And a young one."

"You do not look so young," he says. His lips twitch, as though this discussion of young and old amuses him.

"Things are not always as they appear," Ruby says. She stoops and pulls a bunch of white flowers with yellow centers from the neatly laid row of them in her garden. She holds them out to Rapunzel. "You are welcome to return any time. I have plenty."

Rapunzel takes the bunch and, unexpectedly, moves toward Ruby and kisses her cheek. "Thank you," she says.

"Thank you, sorceress," Prince Cole says. He is a head taller than she is, so she must look up to him. His eyes dance. "You are welcome to join us in the village tomorrow afternoon for our daily walk, if you would like."

"I would very much like that," Ruby says. "And my name is Ruby."

Prince Cole nods, his eyes amused again. Rapunzel smiles with shining white teeth, calling forth a vision of Ruby's best friend, Minnie, and summoning a slight tear in the fabric of her heart. She misses them all so much.

The two—prince and village beauty—turn and race one another through the woods, Rapunzel's hair creating a significant disadvantage in the contest.

Ruby watches them, longing spearing through her chest, until they vanish from her view.

Change

It did not take long for Queen Vivian to know that she would bear the king a child. She thought that perhaps this would endear her to the king, for though she worked her magic every opportunity she was given, she could see that the king still held his heart at a great distance. He did not want to spend time with her as she longed to spend time with him. She had been waiting for three very special words, but still she waited.

She thought that news of a child would, perhaps, draw them forth once and for all, and with his admission, she would win his heart. Her magic was of a simplistic and yet complicated nature. Yes, she could sway emotions, but she could never summon love. If love happened to flow from a heart she desired and bind itself to her with the admission of three simple words, that heart would be hers forever.

But when Queen Vivian told King Sebastien that there was to be a child, his face closed up so tightly that she could not read it even a little. She did not have her staff with her, for she had been forgetting many things of late. The midwife who had examined her said it was to be expected for a woman who was with child. Her magic would fade as well, at the same rate the child within her grew.

King Sebastien pursed his lips. His dark eyes flashed anger. She drew back a small step. "Already," he said. "Already you will give up your gift of great magic."

She could not understand why he would believe this such a bad decision. She did not use her magic for important acts, at least not as far as King Sebastien knew. But then she remembered that he, too, would give up his magic. She looked at him and felt a wave of sadness. Magic was what kept him on the throne of Fairendale. Would he have to surrender that as well?

"I am sorry," she whispered. She tried to touch him, but he turned away. The bottom of his staff hit the floor, but nothing happened. He cursed.

"No," he said. "It was not supposed to happen this way."

Queen Vivian took another step back, but the king

did not turn to her. He did not say anything else. He merely stalked away. She stood looking after him.

Perhaps she should have kept this bit of news a secret for a while longer. She had not considered what losing the whole spectrum of magical powers would do to King Sebastien. She had been foolish. But there was nothing to be done. She pressed her hands against her belly and felt the warmth spread through her. This child would be good. She could feel it.

The day came when it was time for Queen Vivian to bear the child. King Sebastien was nowhere to be found, so Queen Vivian lay alone in her bedchambers, awaiting the instructions of her midwife. When it was done and the midwife had departed, Queen Vivian had a lovely red-faced little boy, tucked snugly in her arms.

Queen Vivian held him all that night and into the next morning, but the king still did not come. So Queen Vivian leaned close to her son and whispered, "You shall do great things for the kingdom, Wendell." And that was that. The boy was named.

In the days following Wendell's birth, King Sebastien did, at last, come. He held his boy in his arms, and there was a small smile that played about the sides of his mouth as he looked at the boy. "He will be strapping," he said. "Look at these hands. And the feet as well." When his eyes met Queen Vivian's, they crinkled. She felt hope awaken in her heart again.

King Sebastien often came to see the child after that. He would dine in the nursery with Queen Vivian and Prince Wendell. He would carry the infant in the crook of his arm, walking down the hallways and pointing out the pictures of the past kings of Fairendale. He would watch the baby sleep in Queen Vivian's arms, and while watching he would stroke her hair and kiss the side of her face.

And one night, when the boy was only six weeks old, King Sebastien whispered the words Queen Vivian had waited to hear for so very long. "I love you," he said, before he kissed the top of her head, touched the cheek of the boy, and slipped away. Her smile remained even as she slept, just as his heart would forever remain hers.

The boy, who was given to smiling and cooing and watching the eyes of his mother as she read stories to him, continued to grow, and soon Queen Vivian discovered she was to bear the king another child.

She knew that this second one would not be a magical child. She would raise them both to know the rules and the depths and dangers of magic, of course, but only one would possess the gift. She looked at the baby in her arms and traced the line of his nose and the curve of his cheek and the curl of his ear.

When King Sebastien came to see her that evening, Queen Vivian told him, "There will be another baby soon."

King Sebastien's eyes glittered. "Oh," he said.

"Perhaps we should raise them as twins," she said. This was something she had been considering for quite some time.

King Sebastien furrowed his brow. "Why?" he said.

Queen Vivian looked at the baby in her arms. "So that one will not think he is less than the other," she said. "We would love them the same, of course. But a gift of magic is a very desirable thing."

King Sebastien looked to be thinking, but he said nothing more for the time being. And then, when Queen Vivian had nearly drifted off to sleep herself, the king's voice came to her. "Perhaps they will both have magic," he said.

"But that is impossible," Queen Vivian murmured, her eyes still closed.

"Nothing is impossible, my dear," King Sebastien said. He took the baby from her arms and rocked him gently. "Not for us."

Queen Vivian marveled at the change that had overcome the king. If she did not know better, she might have thought that her magic still had sway over him. But she had a child. And this child, she knew, was a magical one. She could feel it in the warmth of his body. She could smell it on his skin, a sweet, ancient scent that reminded her of apple cider.

Which meant that her magic was utterly and completely gone.

So she chose to believe that the king had begun to not only love her but adore her, without a single shred of magic bending his heart.

Secrets

Before Ruby can leave her abode and travel to the village of Rosehaven the following morning, Rapunzel knocks on her unstable door. It swings open easily. Rapunzel peers inside and smiles when she sees Ruby huddled by a small fire crackling from a pit dug in the ground.

"I did not have anything to do this morning, so I thought perhaps I would visit," Rapunzel says.

"Do you need more chamomile?" Ruby says, confused. No one has ever really sought her out—not even her best friend Minnie, back in Fairendale.

"No," Rapunzel says. "I only wanted to see you."

The words are like small, bright birds flapping around in Ruby's chest. She feels lighter. Happier. She cannot help but grin. "I am glad you have come," she says. Rapunzel's hair shines even in the dim light of the leaning house. Ruby lifts her hand, as though to touch a smooth strand of it, but then she drops it back into her lap. "Your hair is very lovely."

Rapunzel touches the top of her head. "It is the chamomile." Rapunzel's voice is a whisper, and this, Ruby knows, is the secret of the chamomile. It does not preserve Rapunzel's face. It preserves her hair.

She would like to ask more, for curiosity is quite difficult to quell, but before she can arrange the words in just the right way, Rapunzel says, "You are not from Rosehaven." She gestures vaguely. "You speak a bit differently. Where did you live before?"

Ruby hesitates. Rapunzel notices. She says, "You do not have to tell me if you do not want to."

Ruby thinks about this secret. She thinks about secrets in general. They are very heavy things. Perhaps it would feel better to release it into a friend's hands. She studies Rapunzel. Rapunzel studies her hands. Silence sways around them.

Rapunzel is the first to speak. "I know you have come from somewhere. I know you are not as old as you appear. I would like to know how." Her eyes lift to Ruby's, and they are full of something Ruby cannot bear to see. Sadness. Regret. And a touch of fear. "How have you managed to transform yourself? And can you teach me?"

The words hang between them. Ruby's breath catches in her throat.

"But why would you want to transform yourself?" Ruby says. "Why would you want to leave your happy home?"

Rapunzel clenches her hands. A tear runs down her cheek. "It is a very happy home," she says. "But I am a danger to my parents. There are people who come…" She does not finish. She takes a breath and straightens. "Perhaps you would like to braid my hair? People always like to braid my hair."

She removes three large silver pins from her hair, and one of the dozen knots on her head releases. Her hair is much longer than Ruby would have guessed. Ruby gasps.

"I have never cut it," Rapunzel says.

"It is the loveliest hair I have ever seen," Ruby says. Rapunzel smiles sadly.

"Yes," she says. "People come to see it from everywhere. They touch it. And they are changed."

Ruby blinks. "What do you mean changed?" she says.

"Healed," Rapunzel says.

"Healed?"

"Of whatever ails them. They think it is the hair, but

it is not."

"What is it, then?" Ruby says.

"My tears," Rapunzel says.

Ruby does not quite understand. Is it some sort of magic? "But how can tears heal people?" Ruby says. "And why can you not simply tell them?"

"It is much easier to believe that touching hair produces healing than it is that tears could do such miraculous work," Rapunzel says. She sighs. "I cannot bear to see the sick and the wounded. It is my wishing for their health that makes it so. They must only braid a strand of my hair, and I can feel what they feel in its entirety." She looks up through long golden lashes. Her voice softens to a mere whisper. "I know that you are sad. And I would like to heal your sadness. I would like to restore you to your youth."

Rapunzel holds out a strand of her hair, but Ruby does not touch it. She will not touch it, though the longing crawls to her throat. "No," she says. "I will not take this from you."

Rapunzel begins to cry in earnest then, her words tumbling out. "I have borne so much sickness and sorrow in my life," she says. "And people come and they take more from me for a coin or two. And my parents do not know what else to do to pay for our livelihood, and my brother is sick, and I do not have strength enough to heal him without the help of medicine, and my tears are magic, but they have not been magic for him." Ruby feels the wave of Rapunzel's words crash into her, knock her from her feet, and leave her gasping for air. Rapunzel sighs. "That is why I would like to transform myself. I would like to become someone unrecognizable. I would like to heal my brother with every bit of magic I can summon, instead of giving it away to all the others."

"Perhaps I might help your brother," Ruby says. She knows that Healing is complicated work, but she can at least try.

"Oh, no," Rapunzel says. "That would be far too dangerous."

"Dangerous?" Ruby says.

"The king's brother, Prince Dunstan, watches my home," Rapunzel says. "I am promised to his son, Prince Cole, but the agreement was arranged by the king, after a contest he had to determine which maiden in the land was the most beautiful. King Alvin is very kind, if somewhat misguided about women and beauty, but Prince Dunstan is not kind at all. He would do anything to break our arrangement and use me for his own purposes." Rapunzel stares down at her hands. "And there is one more thing." She clears her throat. "I carry within me the possibility of immortality, which I can only gift to one person in my lifetime. Or so a prophetess told my parents when I was a baby. Prince Dunstan somehow knows this. I believe he would like to become immortal so that he can rule the throne of Rosehaven forever." Rapunzel shivers. "It would be a terrible reign."

Ruby tries her best to understand, but there are so many threads. So she settles on one.

"Is Prince Cole a good prince?" she says.

"Oh, very much so," Rapunzel says.

"He does not seem very prince-like," Ruby says. She thinks of the prince's grin.

Rapunzel smiles. "He was not groomed as a prince," she says. "That is why I enjoy his company so much."

"And he is not like his father?" Ruby says. "He does not want your gift of immortality?"

"Prince Cole has a pure heart," Rapunzel says. "His father…" She lets her words trail off.

"Your kingdom sounds as though it is riddled with problems," Ruby says. "As my kingdom was."

"Your kingdom?" Rapunzel says.

A warmth rises up to Ruby's cheeks. She gestures to Rapunzel's hair. "Is it not heavy?"

"Very much so," Rapunzel says.

"Why do you not cut it?" Ruby says. "Surely no one

would notice."

"It was once foretold by a prophet that if I cut my hair, I would lose my powers," Rapunzel says. She stares at the ground with a sullen look. "And no one wants that."

"Except for you," Ruby says. Rapunzel does not answer.

After that, the girls talk of many other, safer, less complicated things. Books, magic, subjects they have studied in their learning. By the time they are finished with their conversation, which lasts for hours and hours, they both believe they were destined to be best friends— one a beautiful twelve-year-old girl and the other an old woman who is really, beneath it all, another beautiful twelve-year-old girl.

They walk into the village arm in arm, looking quite a pair.

This morning brings a letter from a distant land. King Willis is surprised to see a letter, for it has been some months—perhaps even years—since letters passed between the kingdoms—excepting his, of course. Fairendale is the most powerful land in the realm. Its king is permitted many letters.

But he supposes that his most recent letters, which he sent out nearly a week ago and in which he commanded the other, lesser kingdoms to hand over all their children so he could find the lost children of Fairendale at last, might have sparked some interest. Perhaps it is a king or a knight or even a peasant writing him to say that all the missing children have been captured and will be on their way shortly.

He regards the letter with great hope in his heart.

The curse of Fairendale's golden throne—which was not always a curse but is now one that takes the balance of evil and good in a heart and twists it, unbalances it, weights it for a darker purpose—clutches him as closely as its elaborately carved arms. As long as he sits, it will not let him go.

If King Willis were surprised to see a letter addressed to him in the castle's communication basket, he is even more surprised to learn that this letter comes from the king of Guardia, signed "King Wolfe."

King Wolfe. Well. King Willis did not even know the savages had a king at all. He places the letter on the hulking roll of his stomach for a moment, allowing his mind to run away with his thoughts. Is the king a giant, as the stories say all who come from Guardia are? Does the king keep wolves at his side? Does the king have wolves for children? Is he a shape shifter?

King Willis, in his current state and under this current curse, does not much enjoy reading, though he did once upon a time. And because he enjoyed reading once upon a time, he knows the stories. His questions are the right ones. They are the very ones, in fact, that he wrote on a map of the land, back when he planned to search the realm for his banished brother. In his current state, however, he has no memory of making a map, of planning to locate his beloved brother, of saving the kingdom of Fairendale with goodness, strength, and courage.

In recent days, his father, the tyrannical King Sebastien, has wielded his terrorizing influence and intimidation—from behind a magic mirror, no less—to ensure that his son remains…contained.

King Willis tears the wax seal on the letter (it is a wolf, in burnt orange) and unfolds it. The parchment is thick and gray, the very shade one might expect the sky to be in a place like Guardia, where snow falls morning and evening and all the hours in between.

"My dear king," King Willis reads. "I must entreat you to abandon your search for the children of your kingdom and revoke the reward you have offered to all the lands." King Willis allows the letter to drop out of his line of sight for a moment and stares at the back wall of the throne room. He cannot see the outline of the door, for his vision is quite atrocious. But he stares all the same. He is not looking for the door. He is looking for a thought, and he does not need eyesight at all for this.

The thought for which he is looking is this one: *If the king of Guardia is a savage, why would he care about children and rewards?*

And the next thought is even more disconcerting: *If the king of Guardia is* not *a savage, then what else might King Sebastien have lied about?*

King Willis likely does not want to know the answer to this latter question.

The king picks up the letter and continues reading. "Your search and your reward will cause problems for all the children in the realm, and it is nothing more than savagery to bring danger upon the children of a kingdom. Children are the light of kingdoms. Surely you know this, with a son of your own." Here King Willis allows the letter to drop once more. How does the king of Guardia know he has a son?

The thought of his son, who was stolen by the village people weeks ago, pulls at his heart, but King Willis, rather than feel the sorrow, holds up the letter and continues reading. "As the light of kingdoms, I respectfully urge you to let your imprisoned children go, for they are innocent of any wrongdoing. I urge you, also, to withdraw your request for all the children in every kingdom of the realm. This kind of request damages the relations between kingdoms, and I do not think you want to do that."

King Willis permits himself another thought: *It was not a request; it was a command.*

He continues reading. "If you find that you cannot consent to any of these terms, I must warn you that I will be compelled to move. And by move, I mean march toward your land and help you see reason. I await your response eagerly. Respectfully yours, King Wolfe."

King Willis now allows the letter to fall from his hands and rustle to the floor. A cold fear creeps into his chest and dances there. He places his right hand on his chest to still it, but it does not work. The fear remains. The fear dances. King Willis glances toward the mirror, glances toward the floor, glances up at the ceiling, where the eyes of giants, painted in beautiful, gleaming colors, stare back at him.

A question tiptoes into his mind: Does he fear his father more than the giants, or does he fear the giants more than his father? King Willis considers this for a moment, but it is much too complicated for him to figure.

King of Guardia. He would never have supposed Guardia had a king. He stares at his hands. And a king who can write—it is impressive. There are, of course, scribes that kings can use to maintain letters and communication, and there is no way of knowing if this is what King Wolfe has done, but it appears that the king of the north has surprised King Willis already. Who is to say he would not surprise him more?

Had he sent a letter to Guardia? There were six letters in total, sent by pigeon. How many lands are in the realm? King Willis cannot even find the number in the tangled mess of his mind at this present moment. He shakes his head, but the fog does not clear.

King Willis leans over his large stomach and peers at the letter on the floor. He reaches for it, misses, reaches again, misses, and propels himself forward with such a force that he nearly falls out of his throne. There. He has grasped the letter in his hand. He reads it again. He lets it flutter back to the ground.

What had he read about the people of Guardia in the castle's annals? They were uncivilized people, barely people at all. No, no, that is what his father told him. The annals were empty of information about the people of Guardia. At least he had not uncovered any of that information in the small window of time he had studied the lands. He knows it snows every day in Guardia. He knows that the people—or, rather, the giants—wear heavy furs, which make them appear more animal-like than human. He knows that they live in ice-sculpted homes, but even in his studies, he had found no picture of a castle in the land. A king of Guardia would live in a castle, would he not?

There is simply too little information that he knows. He is unable to form any opinion at all. He leans over to look at the letter again. This time it has fallen on its backside, and while he looks, some words appear. He watches them move and fade. There is a message. A magical one, scrawled across the back of the parchment. King Willis leans forward again, this time securing the letter with a single try. He brings it close to his face. The words have faded, but he waits. Perhaps it will write itself again.

And it does.

The letters appear one after another, remaining for a moment and disappearing, on down the line. King Willis watches until the cycle begins again, and then he crumples the letter in his fist.

"I know your secret," the magical writing continues to say, though its paper has crumpled. There is no stopping a magical message. "I know you do not possess the gift of magic. I know your son does not possess it. I know your wife does, but that is no claim to the throne of Fairendale. The magical boy is the true king. Give your people their true king."

It is difficult to describe the feelings that turn the face of King Willis red and then purple and then a pale gray. At first it is anger, the kind that says, *How dare he?* Next it is irritation, which says, *The magical boy is still alive?* And last it is fear, which says, *How does he know?*

His father had been so careful to cover the fingerprints of magic in the castle. The village people had willingly believed that he, King Willis, was the twin of his brother, though his brother was born one year and one day before him. The people had also willingly believed that he, King Willis, possessed the gift of magic, which he then passed on to his son.

None of it was true.

Another fear creeps into the king's throat. His brother. Wendell. What if Wendell is the king of Guardia? Wendell, Wolfe, they are not so very different, are they? King Willis looks around the throne room. He catches sight of the mirror. He rises. He must ask his father. He must tell him what has happened. He must find out what to do.

The problem, if it can be called a problem, is that as soon as King Willis stands, as soon as his connection with the throne is broken, a heaving sorrow slams into his chest. His brother. How he has missed his brother. If Wendell is alive, he must find him. He must bring him back to Fairendale, where they can all live happily ever after.

The throne, behind King Willis, curls a tendril of pale violet magic and wraps around the ankle of the king. The king's heart hardens, momentarily. He will kill his brother when he sees him.

But then it softens again. No. He would never kill his brother. He loves his brother. And the further King Willis walks from the throne the thinner the tendril of violet magic becomes. He walks toward the throne room doors. He will go to the library. He will find his maps. He will search.

Wendell is alive. Still. After all these years.

Come back to me, Wendell, the heart of King Willis sings. *Come back to me. Come back to me. Come back to me.*

The bond between two brothers is beautiful thing.

But before King Willis reaches the throne room doors, the magic mirror shimmers to life, and King Sebastien stands tall and angry inside it. He calls to his son, and King Willis has never done anything but obey his father. So he turns. He walks. He stands before the mirror that holds a man who wears a superficial crown.

"Father," King Willis says. His voice quavers. His father cannot know what he was about to do. King Willis stares into the mirror, and a bravery he has never felt before in his entire life seizes him, shakes him, comes spilling out of him in a gasp, a swell, a pointed movement. He gestures behind him, to the letter that lies on the floor. "You lied to me about the people of Guardia. They are not savages. I have just received a letter from their king."

King Sebastien does not appear surprised in the least. "A letter," he says. "And why would the king of Guardia be writing to you?"

"He is a civilized person," King Willis says, and his voice grows stronger with every word. His back grows straighter. His shoulders grow taller. "He asks that I revoke the reward for the missing children and that I let the imprisoned children go."

King Sebastien laughs, a sound that scrapes against King Willis's ears and drags dagger points down to his chest. "Well, isn't that presumptuous of a king," he says. His eyes harden. "No one tells the king of Fairendale what to do."

"But perhaps he is right in what he says," King Willis

says, but already his voice has grown weaker, his shoulders have slumped slightly forward, his back bends. It is much too heavy a weight to defy his father. How can he be expected to? There is a possible future where his father might not be contained behind the glass of a mirror. What then?

"Many men can appear civilized in a letter," King Sebastien says. "The king of Guardia cares nothing for the children. He only cares for himself, as is true of every king."

No, King Willis would like to say. *No, it is not true of me. I care for my brother. I care for Clarion. I care for my son. I care for you, Father. Or I did.*

But, then, he is not really a king—or should not be, anyway.

"Why do you think your brother left you?" King Sebastien says. His eyes flash. King Willis feels the words wrap around his heart and squeeze.

"He knows our secret," King Willis continues, deflecting. His voice shakes. "He says he will march against us if the throne is not returned to its rightful king."

This is not exactly what King Wolfe wrote in his letter, but the pieces have become jumbled in the mind of King Willis.

King Sebastien waves his hand. "Do not concern yourself with what that savage king says—though it might be worthwhile to build your army."

"I have no resources to build an army," King Willis says, and his shoulders slump more. It is his fault. He has no men because he ordered them to follow the fleeing children of Fairendale, and an entire army died in the dragon lands, by dragon fire.

"Then you must gather one," King Sebastien says. "As I did in my day."

King Willis raises his eyes to his father. King Sebastien, though graying around the edges of his hair, is still strong and capable and very handsome. King Willis can see why people would have followed his father into a battle only one would win. But how can King Willis gather an army? He has nothing to promise them but himself. And what is that worth?

The broken king shakes his head. "I cannot," he says. "I do not have it in me."

King Sebastien growls, and the sound of it shakes King Willis, rattling his teeth in his mouth. "Do not tell me you do not have it in you," King Sebastien says, his words now slow and measured. As he speaks, a cloud of bright blue mist reaches from the mirror and wraps around King Willis. "You are my son."

The mist swirls and thickens, until King Willis cannot be seen at all, until he, inside it, can see nothing but a cloud. And then, as quickly as it appeared, the mist disappears, entering every opening in his head—ears, eyes, nose, mouth. It is as though the blue mist becomes King Willis.

King Willis, with a cloud of blue within, rearranges his shoulders once more. He lifts his chin. He clears his throat. "I can," he says. And then louder, "I can."

He does not even consider where an army might come from, but he does not need to figure this out today. Today is for knowing that he can.

"I can," he says again, and then he laughs, a laugh that sounds nothing like one King Willis would utter. In fact, it sounds more like a laugh that belongs to his father —low and hollow and sharpened with a thousand sword points.

"You will keep the throne at all costs," King Sebastien says.

"I can," King Willis says.

"You will gather an army that will fight for Fairendale," King Sebastien says.

"I can," King Willis says, louder this time.

"You will kill your brother if he dares move against you," King Sebastien says.

"I c—" Here is where King Willis falters.

King Sebastien's eyes narrow. "You will kill your brother if he dares move against you," he says again.

King Willis hesitates for the smallest moment in time. His brother. Will this cost him his brother? Would Wendell not be better suited for this throne, with his wise mind and compassionate heart?

"You will kill your brother if he dares move against you!" King Sebastien shouts. The blue mist has begun growing again. It wraps around King Willis's ankles and legs.

"I can," King Willis says, and the mist dissipates, taking with it all hesitation, contemplation, and adoration.

Garth bursts through the door at that moment. King Willis spins around, momentarily unsteady, but the boy puts out his hand and helps his king regain his composure. "Lay the table for Queen Clarion and me," King Willis says. "We shall dine within the hour."

Perhaps it is time to demand some answers from his queen.

It might surprise the king to know that Queen

Clarion has been inside the throne room this entire time. She has seen it all. She has seen the letter. She has seen the frightening appearance of King Willis's father in the mirror, something that very nearly made her gasp and rush forward to save her husband. She has seen the hesitation and wondered at it.

She heard the words King Willis read aloud from the ivory parchment, and her heart shored itself up. Perhaps she could ask for help. Perhaps she could send a letter of her own. The plans began spinning in her mind, just before a blue cloud surrounded King Willis and cut him off from her view. She pressed her hands against her mouth to keep the scream inside.

She has not, alas, seen the magical message, so while she retires to the castle library, to await the supper she will eat with King Willis, she thinks only of writing to the king of Guardia.

The king of Guardia. She had no idea.

Queen Clarion spends a great many minutes searching through books on the lands of the realm. She can find nothing about a king of Guardia. Most of the books say that the people of Guardia are elusive, and those who enter the land very rarely come back out. Surely the land sent a prophet to share a Vision about her son, Prince Virgil, and his lack of the magical gift, as the other lands did throughout the years. Perhaps she can visit the dungeons beneath the dungeons after she dines with the king, since that is where many, if not most, of the prophets in the land are now kept, for their unfavorable Visions.

When the hour is half past, and she still has half an hour to herself before she will be summoned to dine, she slips on silent feet back to the throne room. She peers through the back passage, which she had used before to enter unseen by King Willis. The king is not on his throne. The letter, crumpled, still remains at the foot of it. She looks toward the entrance, to the mirror, behind her, and then she steals inside and picks up the letter. She reads it for herself, and she cannot help the smile that stretches her lips, a smile that feels like hope.

She will dine with the king, and she will convince him that the king of Guardia is correct. She will break the hold that the blue cloud of magic presumes to have on her husband. She knows that he loves. She knows that the king still feels in his heart, and she will appeal to that heart. She will nurture it. She will unbind it from the shackles that hold it down in the worst kind of subjugation known to man.

Queen Clarion walks toward the mirror. It does not shimmer to life. She only sees herself in it, a pale face with hollow eyes. The crown on her head sparkles in the torch light. Its red, blue, and green gems dance. She removes the crown from her head and stares at it. It is a beautiful piece of art. But she does not need it. She would not need to wear it on her head to be happy. She has need only of her son, only of her husband, only of the man, the long-lost prince, she has come to see as a brother who once soothed a lonely heart and showed it how to love. She places the crown back on her head and turns to go, but as she turns the letter in her hand crackles, a sound that startles her so absolutely that she drops it. She bends to pick it up, and that is when she notices the magical message on the back. As it rhythmically writes its message and the message slowly vanishes, Queen Clarion brings her hand to her mouth. Her heart beats fast and heavy and loud. A roar fills her ears.

No. She has never told anyone. It cannot be.

Has the king read these words? Could this be why he would like to dine with her this eve in so formal a place as his dining hall, when they have spent the last several suppers in his chambers?

Queen Clarion places the letter back at the foot of the throne. She takes a deep breath and lets it out slowly. It does not change anything. She will still appeal to the king's humanity, which she knows remains, even after a blue cloud and an impossible conversation with his father in a magic mirror. Humanity will win over power. It must be true. It must. King Willis is a broken man, a man pulled apart by his father and put back together crooked. But he can be mended. We can all be mended. We have only to desire it in our deepest places, which then makes it possible for the mending to begin. Or so Queen Clarion believes.

She glances back at the throne and the mirror. In the meantime, she will continue searching for a way to be rid of both of these curses.

A bell rings out, a loud, clanging one that indicates the serving of a meal in the castle. Queen Clarion rushes from the throne room and out into the hallway. She did not intend to remain as long as she did, but it appears that no one is around to see her emerge. She can hear the king at the other end of the hall, not yet around the slight curve of wall where she could see him. She ducks into the dining hall, for a moment to think.

The table is set in an uncustomary way. Rather than two bowls set at opposite ends of the very long table, there is one bowl at one end and another bowl at the elbow of this seat. Queen Clarion is rather glad for this; it means that they will not have to shout across the table, as they have done on other occasions when the king invited her to dine. It is awkward to sit at such a large table and not be able to hear one another speak.

She sits in the elbow seat. The king shuffles in, his back straighter than she has seen it in a very long time. She feels a prick of unease. She saw the cloud. She saw what happened when King Willis emerged. She saw the blue mist soak into his eyes. Perhaps humanity is not enough when one is blinded.

"Well," King Willis says. He smiles at her, and the unease grows. It is not a King Willis smile. This one is hard around its edges. It is the kind of smile she remembers from his father. "I see I have left you waiting."

"Not so very long," she says, for lack of anything better to say. She ponders, considering what she has learned from the Old Man's Great Book. She has seen nothing of a spell that would allow a person to use a mist to inhabit another person.

(Allow me a moment of explanation, dear reader. This particular spell does exist, though it is only a very slight possibility that a sorcerer would use it. The spell is not an easy one, and it is not without great personal sacrifice—as in, a piece of one's soul sacrificed to magic, which always tends toward the dark—that it can be done at all. The reason Queen Clarion has not yet read anything about it is that the only information about this particular spell in the Old Man's Great Book resides in a footnote on the very last page. This is for a simple reason: teachers never wanted their students to know about it at all. It is the darkest of the dark magic available, and most teachers would rather pretend it does not exist at all.

It is, as yet, unclear whether King Sebastien has used this spell on his son.)

As Queen Clarion stares at King Willis, she is alarmed by how much he has altered. Is it her imagination? Is she simply more sensitive to the change because of what she has seen?

She will have to consult the Great Book again this eve.

Perhaps it is because the queen is worrying over unknown spells and frightening possibilities that she blurts out, somewhat frantically, "The throne. It is an evil influence. You must not sit on it."

She had not planned to approach this subject as she has, but it is too late to take back hasty words.

The king looks at her, one eyebrow raised in a way she distinctly remembers was his father's way of discrediting someone—usually her. So she tries another approach. "You have no men who will fight for you. Why do you suppose that is?"

She regrets these words, too. She cannot seem to get a handle on her thoughts and the way they move from her mind to her mouth. Anger warms her cheeks, quickly swallowed by shame, and then anger breaks free once more. She had high hopes for King Willis. When his father died, she thought that he might become more like the old King Willis, the one who agonized and planned and searched and acted. Instead, he became spineless, ruthless, utterly unknown. When she looks at him, now, she can hardly see the old Willis. She must summon him from his hiding place. He is there somewhere. She can feel it. He is calling out for help. Something flickers in his eyes, but then it is extinguished by a flash of fury.

"You will not dine with me if you cannot control yourself," he says, his voice hard as the wooden table on which her elbows rest.

"I am sorry," she says, so quietly that the room stills for a moment. She stares at the bowl of soup that she has not touched. "Perhaps we can solve the problems of this kingdom another way, besides building an army."

The king does not ask how she knows he is planning to build an army. Perhaps he has forgotten that he has not mentioned it to her. "What way?" he says. "There is no other way."

"Let the children go," Queen Clarion says. "No one

ever marched against us until we rounded up the kingdom's children." She places a hand on her husband's arm. "Have you seen the kingdom lately, Willis? Have you seen its people? They are empty. The skies are gray. The sun does not shine. The flowers wilt. The grass yellows and dries out. Our beautiful land is dying." Her eyes fill and spill, dripping onto the table.

"I will never let the children go," King Willis says. His voice has softened slightly, and Queen Clarion raises her eyes to his. "They do not deserve to be let go."

Queen Clarion shakes her head. "Then I fear we will never see our son again," she says.

The king is quiet for a moment. He appears to be thinking. Queen Clarion uses this to her advantage. "What if no one wants to steal a throne at all?" she says. "What if it was all in our imagination? What if someone wanted us to believe that the throne was in danger, when it was never in danger at all? What if we found Wendell? What if he came back?"

She has no idea the effect of her words on the king. She does not even look at his face as she says them, so afraid she is of his heavy hand. She braces herself for the pain, but it does not come. And when she looks up again, the king is staring at her with eyes that are golden brown. Her heart warms.

"Willis," she says, taking his hand.

"Clarion," he says, squeezing hers.

They stare. They say nothing. And then a shadow crosses the king's face. It moves up and into his eyes, a small black speck. "You have the gift of magic," he says. His fingers twitch in hers. "You did not tell me."

She drops her eyes to their interlocked hands. "I did not," she says. She cares not who hears it. "I do not know why it did not pass to our son."

"You did not tell me," King Willis says. "All this time I thought it was my fault that our son was born without magic." His hand closes on hers, and this time the grip is painful. She tries to take hers away, but he will not let her. Fear blooms in her chest.

"Let me go," she says.

"I should throw you in the dungeons with the rest of them," King Willis growls. "What did you hope to do with your magic? Steal my throne?"

"I am your wife," Queen Clarion says. Her voice trips and falls and returns to its feet only to trip and fall again. "I do not desire a throne. I do not need one to be perfectly happy. I need you and Virgil and a place where we can live and love and—" But she does not get an opportunity to finish.

"Get out!" King Willis roars. "I have no wish to dine

with you." And he flings away her hand with a harsh growl. She topples backward in her chair, but Garth appears behind her and catches her, pulls her to her feet, and half-carries her toward the door.

"You cannot remain," Garth whispers. "He is not himself."

No. King Willis is not himself. He has become his father.

Queen Clarion looks back at King Willis one final time. And as she watches, his hand rises to his forehead, his shoulders slump, and a single tear drops onto the table.

Vision

The kingdom of Fairendale grew quite busy just after Queen Vivian told King Sebastien of the second child's existence. There were traders to welcome and business to attend, and King Sebastien was gone for many days at a time. Since Prince Wendell could not yet be without his mother, it was not often that Queen Vivian saw her husband.

One day, when Prince Wendell was sleeping soundly in her bedchambers, Queen Vivian, in stockinged feet, passed near the throne room. The door at the back of the throne room, the one that led into a small passage that led directly to the dining hall, was left ajar, and she stood beside it, hoping for a glimpse of the king she missed. She hoped for a sighting of anyone, actually, for Queen Vivian was the sort of woman who enjoyed the company of others, who came alive in the middle of a crowd, and it had been much too long since she had attended a dignified dinner or even welcomed guests to the castle. Her maidservant did not speak much anymore, for Prince Wendell always seemed to be sleeping when she came to check on her queen. The only conversation Queen Vivian had at any moment in time was with a small baby.

The people of the castle, when she passed on her jaunts down the hallways, always spoke to her in muted tones, as if they were afraid of the baby. She had felt the change, and she did not understand it. Perhaps her magic had held more sway than she had realized.

She very nearly touched the doorknob of this back entrance into the throne room so that she could walk in, unannounced, on her king, but at the precise moment she reached for it, she heard another voice inside the room. It was old and rough, one she did not recognize. She could not hear what this voice said with the door in her way, so she gently pushed it a bit farther away from her, holding her breath in hopes that it would not make a sound. The king, she saw, was focused on the man before him. The man was dressed in a dark brown robe that reached his feet and had wide, hanging sleeves and a hood that covered his head. But even with the hood, Queen Vivian could see the pale skin of his face and the pale blue of his eyes from where she stood; his other features had a blurry quality about them, however, as though an enchantment covered their clarity. A Mask spell? She could not tell for sure.

He held a walking stick that rose nearly to his chest. She flipped through the pictures stored in her mind, taken from the books about prophets in the castle library. This man had the look of a prophet, but he did not look like any of those depicted in the books. Perhaps he was a new, or, rather, unknown one.

Queen Vivian considered the shadows that were always long and wide in the throne room, since King Sebastien did not often light the torches along the back wall. It would be quite easy for her to hide in them. And this is precisely what she did.

She held her breath, slipped past the door and then pressed herself as flat as she could against the throne room wall, though the baby in her belly would not flatten, of course. Her dress did not rustle. Her feet carried no noise. She hardly even breathed.

The king did not look her way.

"Your life remains in danger," the prophet said. His voice crackled as though it had not been used in quite some time.

"I am perfectly safe here," the king said. Queen Vivian closed her eyes. She could feel the apprehension in the king's heart. She could feel that he was afraid. She opened her eyes again and moved them back to the prophet. Was he a danger to King Sebastien? Why was the king afraid?

"There are many who do not wish you to continue ruling this throne," the prophet said. "There are some who would like to see you die."

Queen Vivian tried to keep her breath even. Her son. What would she do if the king died and his killer came for her son? For her and the child she carried? She wanted to rush forward, toward her husband, but something stayed her legs.

"I sent for you to ask whether your original prophecy had changed," King Sebastien said. His voice was hard but steady.

"You will still die by the beak of a blackbird," the prophet said.

Queen Vivian nearly cried out.

"So it has not changed in all these months," King Sebastien said. "Though I have had one child and will soon have two."

"You cannot change death," the prophet said.

"Ah," King Sebastien said. "But I have changed life,

which changes death."

The prophet smiled but shook his head. "You only delay it," he said. "And you endanger your queen."

"My queen?" King Sebastien said. "What of her?"

Queen Vivian heard the note of fear return to his voice. She felt its cold shiver into her heart.

The prophet bowed. "I am only permitted to share a Vision with those whom they concern."

"A Vision concerning my queen concerns me as well," King Sebastien said. His voice was louder now, angry.

"Perhaps if the queen were here," the prophet said. Queen Vivian pressed herself harder against the wall. She did not want the king to see her.

King Sebastien's shoulders slumped. He shook his head. "When will it happen?" he said.

"Your death?" the prophet said.

"Yes," the king said. The word held a weariness Queen Vivian had not ever seen from King Sebastien.

"It is impossible to know this, Your Highness," the prophet said. "I can See a year into the future. It does not happen within the year."

King Sebastien's head tilted. "If you can only See a year into the future, how do you know it will happen at all?"

The prophet smiled at the king, and Queen Vivian thought she detected a bit of sadness in the smile. She closed her eyes and felt. Yes. It was, indeed, sadness. "A prophet does not need to know when to know what," the prophet said.

"When you first came to me, you told me I would be permitted to raise my son," King Sebastien said. "And now I shall have two of them. Will I be permitted to raise them both?"

The prophet shook his head. "I do not know, Your Grace," he said.

King Sebastien ran his hand through his hair, which made the graying tufts stand up. "Is there no way to prevent it?" he said. Desperation latched onto the words and twisted them in Queen Vivian's heart.

"You must take what is given you," the prophet said. But he hesitated and then cleared his throat. "Perhaps if the blackbird is captured you might…" But he did not finish. His eyes had taken on an empty look.

"How does one go about capturing a blackbird?" the king said. Queen Vivian, at that very moment, was wondering the same thing. There were many blackbirds in the kingdom. How would one even know which was the bird that would kill the king?

"She has not yet been born," the prophet said. His

blue eyes had grown quite dark and inky now.

"She," the king said. He laughed a hollow laugh and shook his head. "Perhaps you have been a prophet for too long."

The prophet's eyes cleared again. "Yes, well," he said. "Perhaps I have." He pulled his robe tighter around him and cinched the bit of rope that wrapped around his thin belly. "I have a long journey home. I must take leave of you now." He turned, as if to go, and then he looked back. His eyes had grown soft and sad again. "You must take care," he said. "Be forever on your guard."

"I shall have my men about me at all times," King Sebastien said. The prophet made to leave once more, but the king stopped him. "Who are you?" he said. "I would like to know the one who has brought me news of the future."

The prophet seemed to consider this for a moment. His mouth formed into a word, but he did not say it. Queen Vivian closed her eyes once more, and the prophet's sorrow barreled into her so that she had to open her eyes quickly, for she did not want to cry out. "I am called Jem," the prophet said. He stared at the king for a moment, and then he seemed to wilt a bit more, as if looking on the king was enough to bend his back. "You have loved," the prophet said softly. "Perhaps that is enough."

The king stood. "What is it you say?" he said. The prophet had whispered the words, and perhaps the king had not heard him at all. But Queen Vivian had, and she nodded. Yes. Perhaps love would change everything.

At that very moment, the eyes of the prophet turned to her. The king did not follow the prophet's gaze, but Queen Vivian could see that the prophet knew she was there, had known she was there all along. He looked at her, and the whole world flashed for a moment and then shimmered into a sparkle, and she felt that perhaps she did not know how everything would turn out, but she knew it would be good. Her boys would be strong. She and King Sebastien would be strong.

Queen Vivian patted her stomach, and under the cover of the prophet's shuffling steps, she slipped from the room and padded back down the hallway to her bedchambers, where Prince Wendell was still sleeping.

Unexpected

Sir Greyson, former captain of the king's guard for Fairendale, can bear the silence no longer. He searches the village for Cora. She is not in her house, but he spots her on her way inside the secret passageway beneath the village fountains, almost by accident.

He has come because of a dream.

"Cora," he says. His voice fractures around her name. Her head turns in his direction, acknowledging that she has heard him. Her eyes are cold.

"I thought perhaps you had returned to your king," she says.

He will not allow her to waylay him when he has some very important things to say. "I have had a dream," he says. "Perhaps it is a Vision."

Cora tilts her head at him but does not say anything.

"I have seen you," he says. "You were a blackbird. You were—" He chokes. He cannot say the word aloud.

"Dead," she says for him.

"Yes," he says, his voice hardly a whisper. He reaches for her hand, but she takes a step back. And then she laughs.

"Perhaps it is a symbolic dream," she says. "Perhaps the Cora you saw dead on the ground was the Cora you yourself fashioned in your own mind and heart." The cruel words twist on the wind of her breath. "Do not concern yourself with my well being any longer."

"But I do," Sir Greyson says. "I will." And then: "It is what love does."

"Love," Cora says, her lips turned up in a sneer. "You love your good version of me, who only lives in your mind. That is not love. That is…" She shakes her head. The silence stretches while she tries to find the right word. She lets out a breath when she cannot.

"I love every part of you," Sir Greyson says. "And I have come to say that wherever you go, I will go, too." He bows at the waist, not meeting her eyes.

"I do not need you." Cora grits the words between her teeth, and he feels them clamp around his chest and shake. "I have never needed you."

She begins to move away, but the sorrow in Sir

Greyson will not let her go so easily. "Please," Sir Greyson says. "Lead the people in a way that is right and true and just. Lead them to goodness."

Cora turns slowly back around. "I lead them to justice and safety and—"

"Revenge," Sir Greyson interrupts. "Revenge is never justified. Revenge is never good. Revenge is selfish and unwarranted and dangerous. It will only end in death."

"Perhaps," Cora says. "But the death will be worth it."

"I have seen you in my dream," Sir Greyson says.

"A dream means nothing," Cora says. "A dream is not a Vision. It is not a glimpse of what is to come. It would take very strong magic to kill a sorceress like me." She straightens her back. "Must I remind you that I am a shape shifter?"

Sir Greyson drops his head. "No," he says.

"Perhaps you should run along to the castle, then," Cora says. "Warn your king what is coming." Her eyes blaze into his when he meets them.

"Please do not do this, Cora," he says.

"I do what I must," she says. She lifts her arms and gestures to the gray world around her, as if magnanimously inviting all to agree. "I do what is best for the land and for the realm." Her eyes narrow. "Trust me." And she lunges toward him.

He instinctively reaches for his sword. Cora laughs as she dances away from him. "It is as I thought," she says. "You do not trust me. You never shall again."

"You lunged for me," he says. "It was not a fair test of my trust."

Cora dips her head toward his sword. "And that sword is the only thing that can kill a shape shifter," she says. She vanishes beneath the ground before he can even grasp another word.

He stares down at his sword, still drawn in his hand. Dread barrels his way. He returns the sword to its scabbard and stares at the ground. And then he drops to his knees.

Cora is alone in the secret room beneath the fountains of Fairendale. The torches flicker upon her entrance, as if there is a storm winding inside the room. She is the storm. She watches the effect of her emotions, casting the tables and chairs and corners in eerie, jumping shadows. She winces every time a shadow reaches her face and retreats.

Sir Greyson's dream has deeply unsettled her, though

she would not admit it to him or to anyone else. It is true that the only sword that can kill a shape shifter is his. So that provokes a question: Is it Sir Greyson who will kill her?

Cora shakes off the heavy weight of this wondering. She turns to the blackbird that is a prince. She sits on the bench beside the window where he perches. She offers her first finger, and he grasps it. She strokes his head and his back.

"Perhaps it is time to return you," she says. "Perhaps it is time to make a different plan."

She has, in truth, felt unsettled for quite some time. She cannot shake the feeling that there is someone else making the plans, urging her to move, showing her where to go. And this ignites her anger and, also, her fear. She will move where she must, not where someone would make her.

Cora wriggles her fingers, and the wooden ring that wraps the third finger of her left hand drops into her lap. She touches it, and it slowly grows into a staff. "Now, then," she says. "Perhaps we will try something different."

She weaves a new spell around him, one that she found scrawled on a piece of Mercy's crumpled-up papers. She touches her staff to the bird's head and says the words as they were written. Nothing happens, however. She says them again. And again. And again.

The blackbird does not return to his boy form. Cora's shoulders heave forward, and the breath comes out of her in a whoosh.

The blackbird screeches, an agitated sound. Cora throws her staff to the ground with such force that it pulls all the flames of the torches with it. The room is bathed in sudden darkness.

The blackbird screeches again, and Cora flings it from her hand, runs toward the direction she knows the door to be, picks up the staff that glows in the dark, and bursts through the secret passageway, out into the gray light of a disappointing afternoon. She does not stop once she emerges. She twists on the air, diminishing piece by piece and limb by limb until there is nothing that remains but a blackbird with a wooden ring around one talon.

Her beating wings will beat the doubts away.

The three blind mice have gone in search of news, and it is not long before they return to the children and the prophets in the dungeons beneath the dungeons.

"We have some news," Gus says.

"You might not want to hear the news," says Timmy.

Florence grunts.

Yerin's cloak whispers as he shifts. "What is this news?" he says.

"First, some light," Gus says, and the dark dungeons explode in a splash of match light and then candlelight. The mice throw monstrous shadows against the back wall that would frighten the children if they could not see the three blind mice, pale and shining, in front of them.

"However did you manage to bring us a candle?" Agnes says. "It must be three times the size you are." She laughs, a jolly sound that rings out into the dank cells. "Though I cannot see it."

"Mice have their ways," Gus says. "We can carry many things across long and arduous distances."

"It is most impressive," Agnes says. The mouse bows slightly.

"And the news?" Yerin says.

"The news," Gus says. Some of the children behind Yerin stir and sit up and stand, even. Hope brings strength, you see.

Gus slides through the bars, dragging with him the lit candle, which catches two times on the bars and singes the fur on his shoulder once before he finally wrestles it through. Timmy rolls the candle holder. Yerin sets the candle in the middle of the circle, where children watch the mice with glassy eyes. The other prophets, lying in the back of the cell, do not stir. Yerin does not believe them dead, only asleep. He hopes that they will sleep until they are free. He hopes that when they are free, they will rise again and walk. He hopes…

Well, he should not think about the prophets at this moment. He turns his attention to the mice, who have entered the circle unintentionally formed by the children and Yerin and a glowing candle.

Gus taps his walking stick on the stone. He clears his throat. The children lean forward. Yerin finds himself leaning forward as well, and he nearly laughs at himself but instead presses his hand against his lips.

"The king has offered a reward," Gus says, "for anyone who turns over to him a child."

"A reward," Agnes says. "For the magical children?"

"For every child," Gus says. "For every child in every kingdom, the king will give a handsome reward."

"Every child," Agnes says. "Even those of other kingdoms?"

"Every child," Gus says.

"But surely the people of the realm will not be bought with a reward," Agnes says. "They would be sacrificing their own children."

"Hunger and cold make men do many things," Yerin says.

"But there is no hunger and cold in the other lands," Agnes says. "They are good and beautiful."

"Much has happened to the realm since the days of stories," Yerin says. "Much that you in Fairendale cannot know and see."

"What?" Agnes says. "What has happened?"

"Did the people of Fairendale go to bed hungry in the stories of the land?" Yerin says.

"No," Agnes says.

"And did the people of Fairendale go to bed hungry when you lived among them?" Yerin says.

Agnes considers this. "At times," she says. "But we shared what we had."

"It is not so in most other lands," Yerin says. "The people do not share. There is a wide difference between rich and poor, and no shades in between." Yerin takes a long breath and releases it. "Under the rule of King Willis and his father before him, Fairendale is going the same way."

"And now the children," Agnes says. Her eyes mist. "They will all…" She does not finish.

"Children are the light of a kingdom," Yerin says. "A

kingdom without children is one that cannot stand."

They are all quiet in the dungeons beneath the dungeons, all considering their own pasts and presents and futures. Yerin interrupts the silence with a question. "Have any children been brought to the king?" he says.

Please, no. Please, no. Please, no, his heart says.

"No," Gus says. "Not yet."

Yerin's head drops to his chest. Perhaps the people will prevail against gold. Perhaps he might be given some time. Perhaps he could attempt his One Last Great Act five moons early. Perhaps the universe of magic would permit it, for the sake of sacrifice and ultimate restoration. He could escape from the prison. He could explain everything to the king. He could change the king's mind, he could save the children, he could tell them all what he had Seen in his Visions before…

But he knows that the universe of magic has rules, and these rules say that he will not be given a dose of magic until his birthing day comes. And it is much too distant to change the king's mind about this reward.

How many more children will be joining them? Yerin cannot See.

Yerin lives in this dungeon with a thousand regrets. A dungeon is a most proper place for a man to wrestle with regret, for it is dark and dank, much like regrets.

Why would a good man like Yerin have regrets? Well, dear reader, it must be said that we all have our secrets, we all have our regrets, we all have something we might change in our lives if given the chance to turn back the forward motion of time. Before Aleen, Yerin was the last prophet to travel to the land of Fairendale with a Message for the king. He should have shared his secrets then. He did not expect to find himself in a prison, though there were rumors all over the land about the prophets who had gone missing.

The prophets who, like him, were thrown into this dungeon after carrying their Message to the king.

The land has been dying for a very long time. Yerin should have seen this and now, trapped in a dark and musty dungeon, he regrets having never told what he has been given to carry.

An idea tiptoes into his mind. What if?

It is one of the most brazen and yet auspicious questions to ask, and Yerin, his bones aching against a hard stone floor, dares to ask it of himself.

What if a mouse carried a message to a king? What if a king learned the truth? What if a message and the truth could restore Fairendale to the former days of glory and beauty and shining, shimmering color, thus restoring every other kingdom in the land?

What if?

"Gus," Yerin says.

"Yerin," Gus says.

"Might you be able to secure me some parchment and a bit of ink with a quill pen on your next visit above the dungeons?"

"A mouse can carry many arbitrary and eccentric items across long and arduous distances," Gus says.

"He has been reading in the castle library," Timmy says. "He is fascinated by large words, especially if they are new."

Florence grunts.

"The library?" Agnes says, hope lifting her voice. "Might you bring us a storybook?"

The mouse clears his throat. "Alas, I believe a book might prove too heavy for this mouse," he says. "Perhaps mice cannot carry everything."

There is a book that might help them. A book made of brown leather, with golden flourishes and red jewels affixed to its cover. But Yerin thinks a letter might be better. There is no guarantee that the book could help; magic and the book most certainly would. But there is no magic here in this dungeon.

Gus turns in Yerin's general direction. "I can bring parchment and a quill. For a letter?"

"Yes," Yerin says. "A very important one."

"I will do this." Gus begins to turn.

"There was one other thing," Timmy says. "You told me to remind you, and I am doing so now."

"What is it?" Gus says. His whiskers twitch.

"A letter?" Timmy says. "A letter has come?"

"Ah, yes," Gus says. "A letter. The king has received a letter from the kingdom of Guardia. Do you know the kingdom of Guardia?"

"Guardia," Agnes whispers. "The land of giants and savages."

"Yes, I believe that is the one," Gus says. "I overheard the king tell a man that he had received a letter from the king of Guardia. I believe the king called this king of Guardia civilized. Was that the word?" Gus turns in Timmy's direction.

"Yes, precisely," Timmy says.

Florence grunts.

"Civilized," Agnes says, her voice swelling in wonder. "The king of Guardia, civilized."

But Yerin is not caught on the terminology of the king or even that the king of Guardia sent King Willis a letter. Something else has disturbed him far more than all that.

"You said you overheard the king tell a man," Yerin

says. "Who was this man?"

"Alas, I do not know," Gus says. "I could not see."

Agnes giggles.

"But you could hear," Yerin says. "The boy told us all the servants had left the castle."

"Perhaps all the servants have left the castle," Gus says. "But this man was no servant."

"A soldier?" Yerin says.

"No," Gus says.

"And how do you know?" Yerin says.

"The man told the king that he must—no, he would —kill his brother when the time came," Gus says. "I do not believe servants or soldiers can give orders to a king."

"No," Yerin says, his voice barely a whisper. "They cannot."

"The king of Guardia promised the king of Fairendale that he would march against him if the king of Fairendale did not revoke the reward," Gus says.

"The giants will come?" Agnes says. She clasps her hands together. "Perhaps they are the ones to save us."

"The stories do not speak well of giants, child," Yerin says. Sometimes a man is unable to keep his dark thoughts to himself in the face of such hope that will surely be disappointed. He would never wish the giants to come their way. Giants have never brought goodness upon a land, only destruction.

"The man who spoke to the king advised him—" Gus begins.

"Ordered him," Timmy says.

Gus thrusts out his walking stick, but Timmy is nowhere around him. The force with which Gus thrusts, the force that is unmet by a mouse leg, for which he had intended this blow, makes him spin in place. "Now, then," Gus says when he has stopped spinning. "The man who spoke to the king ordered him to build his own army."

"So they will go to war," Yerin says. "Over the children."

"You are the prophet," Gus says. "Tell us what you See."

"I See nothing," Yerin says. "I See only fog."

"The future is changing," Gus says. "That is why prophets See fog, is it not?"

Yerin shakes his head. He does not know. He has always been able to See the future, though the distance of that future has changed in all the years he has been a prophet. Sometimes he could See years in advance. Sometimes only days. Now he Sees nothing.

The dungeons grow quiet. Water drips into the bowl Yerin and the children have placed beneath the leak.

"The giants will surely win a war," Agnes says. "They

will make the king see reason. If the king of Guardia has entreated King Willis to let the children of the realm go, surely he feels that way about us, too." The children shift around her. They nod. They let their own hearts warm and swell.

Hope is stubborn and unreasonable. The children have no cause to hope, for it is all speculation. But their hearts do not care.

And even Yerin, who knows the true nature of giants and what might happen if giants invade Fairendale—if the people of Guardia really are giants, that is—feels a surge of warmth in the center of his chest.

The endless, exquisite, effervescent stir of hope.

The bones in the cell beside him begin to shiver.

Calvin carries a very large basket of supplies—a treacherous thing to carry down the steep and narrow stairs that lead to the dungeons beneath the dungeons. And because he nearly toppled into dark nothingness at the top of the stairway and his heart froze into a useless block, he has now changed his tactic. He is a resourceful fourteen-year-old. He drags the large basket behind him. He only hopes that the basket will not fall apart on the way down; that would defeat the purpose of bringing all of this food in one single visit. He would like to deliver it to the children as it is, for this is the largest supply he has ever brought at one time. This is namely because there are no longer guards who stand at the secret door to the dungeons—or where they estimated the secret door to be, since none could actually see it—but it is also because he has worked tirelessly to coax the castle gardens to give him something, *anything*. And today, he brings much bounty. He is quite proud of his efforts, as he should be. Poor Calvin has worked day and night and night and day. He rarely sleeps anymore.

His descent down the stairs makes a dreadful racket. He has a candle lodged between his teeth again. His teeth grip it so tightly he can taste the wax. He wrinkles his nose, but he does not quit. Calvin never quits. Shadows leap and lunge all about him.

In the days since all the king's servants left the castle, Calvin has been free to come down to these dungeons beneath the dungeons any time he desires. But, alas, he is so very busy with other duties around the castle that he is unable to come often. When he does come, however, he no longer feels the need to hide what he brings. No one is watching. He is glad for that, for it allows him a measure of success. For example: today, before dragging this basket through the secret door, Calvin pillaged some empty rooms of the castle. He has brought not just the candle in his mouth but a great many candles piled inside the basket of vegetables. And there are many more rooms. He will pillage them at a later date.

The blind girl will be pleased. Yerin, too, of course, but it is the blind girl's smile—the radiant glow of Agnes —he most wants to see.

When he rounds the last corner before the open chambers that lead to the cells, Calvin sees some large and frightening shadows. Monsters. Are there monsters in the dungeons now?

Something propels him forward, however, though everything in his mind is screaming, *Run.* He cries out in horror, as though stunned that his legs would so betray him, and nearly drops the candle in his surprise. His legs finally catch up with his mind, but because the basket is behind him, he does not make it far. He falls, backward, into the basket, helpless to pull himself out, at least in any life-saving span of time.

"What?" Calvin says around the candle in his mouth. His legs kick and flail. He thrusts his upper half forward, trying to propel himself out of the basket. He squeezes his eyes shut when he realizes his efforts do not produce the result for which he hoped.

"Calvin," Yerin says. "My dear boy."

The voice of the prophet soothes him somewhat. Yerin would not speak so plainly and calmly if there were danger present. Calvin opens his eyes and looks at the ground, which is where he has been trained to look when talking to people. He is surprised to see, before him, three white mice, standing on two feet, wearing dark spectacles.

"Who are you?" one of them says.

"It is a boy," another says.

The third grunts.

The candle drops into Calvin's lap. The corner of his tunic catches fire, but Calvin notices immediately, picks up the candle, and beats out the fire with a towel.

Talking mice. He has never heard of such a thing, except in stories.

He must be dreaming.

"There is nothing to fear," Yerin says. "Calvin, these mice are friends. And they talk."

As if he had not noticed. Calvin stares at the mice.

"How is it…" he says, but he does not finish.

"They are enchanted mice," Agnes says. "Unlike any other."

Agnes smiles in his direction. He notices that her eyes have begun to sink into her face, which is much thinner than it was when he visited days ago. He will have to remedy that, and he has brought enough food to do it.

The food. He must get out of the food. He grips the candle between his teeth again and uses his arms to pull himself out of the basket. He stands but finds that he is slightly dizzy. One hand moves out to the iron bars. Agnes places her hand on top of his.

"You have come," she says. "And you have brought food."

How does she know he has brought food?

"I smell cucumbers," Agnes says.

"Yes," Calvin says. "I have brought some."

"And carrots," Agnes says, her voice growing more excited. Her hand squeezes his. "It will be a feast."

He glances over at the mice and back at Agnes and Yerin. "I am sorry I have been so long."

"You must not apologize," Yerin says. "You work hard. We are…" The prophet does not finish.

Calvin glances at the mice again.

"The mice have agreed to become our eyes and ears of the castle," Yerin says. "Currently, they are tasked with bringing me parchment and a quill."

Calvin tilts his head and looks at the prophet. "Parchment?" he says.

"I must pen a letter," Yerin says. "To help, I hope."

"I can bring parchment on my next visit," Calvin

says. "Garth will know where to find some."

"Garth is a man?" Yerin says. He grips the iron bars tightly enough to drain his knuckles of all color.

"No," Calvin says. "Garth is a boy. Only slightly older than me." The prophet steps back from the bars. "The king has offered a reward for the missing children," Calvin continues, unpacking some of the vegetables and sliding them through the bars.

"Yes," Yerin says. "We have heard this from the mice."

"And the king of Guardia has sent the king a letter."

"This, too, we know," Yerin says.

Calvin does not say anything else as he unpacks the remainder of the basket. When he is finished, Agnes says, "Thank you, Calvin, for bringing us so much."

"I do not know when I will return," Calvin says. "There is much to do, but I try my best not to let you starve."

"You do well," Yerin says. "You must not worry yourself over us."

Calvin dips his head and turns to go, but at the last moment, he spins back around. He glances at the mice, still standing in their same positions, as though they are more a child's toy than real rodents. "They have been here long?" he says.

"We have only just come," one of them says.

"So you know what happens around the castle," Calvin says.

"Somewhat," the same mouse says.

Calvin knows the impossibility of what he asks, but he asks it anyway. "Do you know where the key to the dungeons beneath the dungeons is? I would like to free the children and the prophets."

"We know nothing of a key," the first mouse says.

"But perhaps we can find out," the second one says.

The third mouse grunts.

"We can slip into small spaces," the first mouse says.

"We can look," the second mouse says.

The third mouse says nothing.

Calvin nods and turns away again, but this time he is stopped by the voice of the prophet.

"The bones," Yerin says. "Might you check on the bones, Calvin?"

Calvin had forgotten about the bones. He crosses the stone floor and peers into the neighboring cell. "They are as they were," he says. "Unmoved."

"They have not moved?" Yerin says.

"It does not appear so," Calvin says. He turns back to the prophet, who has a troubled look on his face. "Why?"

"I only thought I heard something this morning…or

evening," Yerin says, his eyes clouded. "It is no matter." He clears his throat. "Has someone been to see the king?"

"No," Calvin says. "No one has visited the castle for quite some time. It is only me, Garth, the queen and king."

"And the prince?" Yerin says.

"He remains missing," Calvin says.

Yerin sighs. Calvin feels its cold wind skip across his back.

"I shall continue my search for the key," Calvin says. He looks at the mice. "Will you tell me if you find anything?"

"We will tell you what we find," the first mouse says.

"Of course," the second one says.

The third one grunts.

With that, Calvin returns up the stairs without a candle to light his path and marvels, momentarily, at the way his feet now seem to move of their own accord, never once tripping on stairs he cannot see.

It is as though he, too, is blind for a moment in time.

On the third day of Ruby and Rapunzel's instant

friendship, Ruby waits in her shelter for Rapunzel. After a time, she emerges into the woods to wait and then moves into her garden. But Rapunzel does not come as she had promised. So Ruby ventures into the village.

Rosehaven is abuzz with the latest news. The king of Fairendale has offered a reward for any and all children. The people, on every corner, talk about how desperately they need this money. They talk about delivering all children to the king of Fairendale. They talk about what they will do with the reward.

For once, Ruby is glad she is living in the body of an old woman.

But Rapunzel. And Prince Cole.

She races toward the castle. She has never been to Rapunzel's house. She does not know where it might be, which is why she heads, instead, to the castle. But on her way, she hears a familiar voice emerging from a tavern. She approaches the doorway and enters. It is Rapunzel's father.

"We have a magical daughter," he is saying. "But she is not from the land of Fairendale."

"It makes no matter," says one of the men gathered in a circle around him. "We demand that you hand her over."

"Never," Rapunzel's father says, and one of the men

forces a fist into his face. For a moment Rapunzel's father looks at her, his head tilted sideways, his eyes so sorrowful that she can feel it in her throat. The moment passes in slow motion, Ruby watching the face of Rapunzel's father twist all the way to the left and then, as though attached to a spring, begin to pull back to the front. The tavern erupts into an explosion of sound. She can hear nothing but a mass of voices, a blur of words, but Ruby reads what is blazing from the eyes of Rapunzel's father.

Go. Find my daughter. Keep her safe.

And Ruby obeys. She runs as fast as she can toward the castle. She hopes that on her way she will find Prince Cole and he will know where Rapunzel is.

She makes it all the way to the stone steps of the castle before she spots the prince, sitting beside Rapunzel on a small stone bench. She cannot even appreciate the luxury of Rosehaven's royal abode, so consumed is she with her important mission.

Rapunzel and Prince Cole stand when she draws nearer. "Ruby," Rapunzel says. "What is it?"

Ruby places her hands on her knees and bends over for a moment. Her breath. If she could only catch her breath.

Prince Cole helps her straighten and pats her back. He looks from Ruby to Rapunzel, his eyes darkening slightly with worry. "Tell us why you are running," he says.

"There is danger," Ruby says. "You must come with me."

"Danger?" Prince Cole says.

"The people," Ruby manages to say without gasping. "They are going to round up all the children of Rosehaven. Just like the king of Fairendale did in my homeland."

"Fairendale," Prince Cole says sharply.

"I will explain it all when you are safe," Ruby says, turning her eyes to Rapunzel. "Please. Come with me."

Rapunzel does not hesitate. She takes Ruby's hand, and they begin to move.

"Wait," Prince Cole says. "You cannot go through the village."

Ruby nods. She had not thought of this. "Then where?" she says.

"This way," Prince Cole says, and he leads them to the back of the castle, where an immaculate garden, arranged in a clever maze, awaits them. Prince Cole calls back over his shoulder. "Follow me and you will not get lost."

They do. The gardens take them all the way to another section of the woods. They circle around the village. It is nearly sunset when they finally reach the home of Ruby.

Prince Cole eyes the leaning structure. "I do not think it will withstand the determination of the people," he says. "We must find a better hiding place."

Ruby paces. She knows he is right. Her lopsided home will never be a good enough hiding place. She searches her mind, trying to locate the enchantments she learned from Arthur in his kitchen, where Maude always offered pumpkin spice cookies sprinkled with sugar. She thinks of the cookies, and her mind fastens on something.

Yes. That is it.

She lifts her staff, touches it to the ground, says the words that seem to come from somewhere far away, from someone else's lips, and there, where a small misshapen rock had been, a gray stone tower begins to rise—mossy on its left side. It shakes the ground as it grows, and Ruby has barely enough time to shout, "Crawl through the window, Rapunzel!" and Rapunzel has barely enough time to do exactly what she says before the tower is much too tall for any to enter or leave. Prince Cole and Ruby, the two left on the ground, stare up at it, in awe.

When it ceases to grow taller, when Rapunzel calls down, "This will do, I think!" Ruby collapses on the ground. Rapunzel shouts down at her, but Prince Cole begs her to be quiet. He drags Ruby into her shelter, promises he will return with a bottle of Rapunzel's tears, and darts out of the clearing, his orange robe clapping the wind behind him.

Rapunzel moves from the window, drops to the stone floor, and covers her face with her hands.

Prophet

Later that eve, while Queen Vivian was tucked away in her chambers, rocking Prince Wendell to sleep, a knock sounded on her door. Thinking it was her maidservant, who usually came by to bring her a bit of food, she said, "Please. Come in." But the eyes that peered at her from the door were the same eyes she had watched in the throne room, hours ago.

The features of the face had cleared a little. She could see the long nose, the bushy black-and-gray eyebrows, the small mouth, turned up at the corners. He looked familiar and unfamiliar at the same time.

She rose.

"Please," the prophet said. "I came only for a moment. Sit and rest."

She did, gladly, for she could not bear to be on her

feet much anymore, as the time of her second child's birth grew nearer.

"I came to see you, for there is a Word you need to hear," he said.

"About the king?" Queen Vivian said. Her heart clenched. She already knew the Word.

"About you," the prophet said. He looked at her so intensely she had to look away. She rested her gaze on her son's angelic face. At last she looked back at the prophet. She met his sparkling blue eyes and noticed the deep wrinkles around them and knew that this prophet had known a merry life. And this made her trust him.

"Very well, then," she said. "Please, sit down."

He sat in a chair next to her bedside, placed his walking stick, which could be mistaken for a magical staff if Queen Vivian did not already know that prophets had no magic, on the floor across his feet, and leaned forward, one gnarled, spotted hand reaching out to stroke her baby's cheek. "He is a very beautiful child," he said.

"Yes," she said. "He looks a bit like his father to me." She had never been this close to a prophet before. She could see the flecks of silver in his blue eyes.

The baby shifted in her arms, yawned, and smacked his lips but did not wake. Queen Vivian kissed his forehead and then lifted her eyes once more to the prophet before her. "What do you wish me to know?" she said, her voice tightening around the words.

"You have the Word I brought the king," the prophet said. "About his death." A pause. "You will die as well." He did not meet her eyes.

Queen Vivian drew in a breath and tried to still her heart. She stared at the prophet, but there was nothing on his face or in his demeanor to alarm her. He was simply an old man. So she said, "We all die at one time or another." She was still quite young, after all.

The prophet met her eyes. "What I have to tell you may seem strange," he said. "But you will soon see that it will all come to pass exactly as I have foretold it."

Queen Vivian could not speak, so she merely waited. The prophet leaned back in his chair and rubbed his hands against the tops of his legs. "You will die," he said. "And someone will try to take you from where you lie. Someone else, who has waited many years for you, will find you, and you will join her sisterhood and become a force of good in our realm."

"A sisterhood," Queen Vivian said. She had never heard of such a thing.

"There will be three of you," the prophet said. "Though, for a time, you will only be two."

"I do not understand," Queen Vivian said. "This is

many years from now, yes?"

The prophet shook his head, and his eyes turned sad. "No, my dear," he said. "You shall die in the birthing of your second son."

"My son," she said, and she looked down at the baby sleeping in her arms. She could not die. Her sons—two of them!—would need her. She could not leave them alone with their father, not without her presence to soften his edges.

The emotion of it all tumbled from her mouth. "But I do not want to die."

"It has already been written," the prophet said. "I have Seen it myself. I have Seen the one who comes to take you for his own purposes. And we are only permitted to rewrite that part of the story, not the one where you die."

She did not know what he was saying, a story that has been written, rewriting only a portion? She could hardly breathe with the weight of his words.

"Do you want to become a force of good in the realm?" the prophet said.

"No," she said. "Not if it means leaving my sons to a future without a mother."

The prophet leaned forward again, and this time his hand moved to Queen Vivian's cheek. His touch was gentle, as a father might touch a child. "My dear," he said. "Your sons will be part of the reason this realm will be saved."

Queen Vivian stared at him.

"I know it is difficult to understand all I speak," the prophet said. His hands, once more, fell to the tops of his legs. "But it is of the utmost importance that you trust me. You know my name."

Yes. She did know his name. This was the single most important thing to know about a prophet. When a name was exchanged between a prophet and a person, the prophet could not lie. She had heard his name spoken in the throne room, where he spoke to King Sebastien. He must have known she was there.

"Jem," she said.

"Yes," he said.

"So I will die," she said. "Soon."

"You will lose your life to give your son life," Jem said. "That is a noble thing."

Queen Vivian felt the tears shored up within her burst to the surface. She could not see the prophet. She could not even see her child. The whole room blurred. When she was finished, the prophet was still there.

"I am sorry I do not bring better news," Jem said.

"You did not tell King Sebastien," she said.

The prophet's eyes turned to glass. She could feel his sadness matching her own. "No," he said. "I did not."

"Why not?" she said.

"I fear it would break our king," he said.

"But he will find out soon enough," she said.

"Perhaps he might be strengthened between now and then," Jem said, and he gave her such a significant look that she felt it pierce all the way down into the deepest parts of her, where her secret lay hidden. He knew. He knew that she could sway the minds of people with her magic. But she did not have any magic left.

Jem touched her arm again, and she felt a hot, scalding wind move through her body. "You have it now," he said.

Queen Vivian gasped. "You…" she said.

Jem nodded once. "I have a power as well," he said. "It only works on the worthy. And it weakens me considerably." He slid from his chair and onto the floor.

"Oh!" Queen Vivian said, and she began to rise from her bed.

"No, my dear," Jem said. "Call the manservant. But allow me a moment before you do."

Queen Vivian peered over the side of her bed, where the prophet appeared to be frozen. Only his mouth and eyes could move, it seemed.

"When you die," he said, "you must concentrate on the task before you."

"My task?" she said. "But I shall be dead."

He continued but did not address her concern. "You must find Good Cheer."

"Good Cheer?" He was speaking in riddles, and Queen Vivian had never liked riddles much. Perhaps, having gifted her, the prophet had then turned mad. She nearly reached for the bell that hung beside her bed.

"Wait," Jem said. "There is more. Good Cheer is a person. She is one of the three Graces, the first. You are the second. Which means you must find Good Cheer." His voice faded a bit. His eyes were flickering closed. "And there is a spell you must perform on the day of your son's birth. It is the only way." He coughed. "It is not a very well known spell. You likely have never heard of it."

"Where can I find the spell?" Queen Vivian said.

"In the castle library, I have left some instructions," Jem said. "And within those instructions is the spell. I trust you will use it well."

Though she had no knowledge of what the prophet spoke, Queen Vivian said, "And what if I do not find Good Cheer?"

"Then the whole realm will be lost," Jem said, his voice rough and soft. Queen Vivian pulled the string.

Someone must help him. He could not die here in her chambers.

"I cannot do it," she whispered, thinking the prophet could not hear her. She clutched Prince Wendell to her chest and kissed his forehead again. His black lashes fluttered on his cheek.

"You have been chosen," the prophet whispered, startling her. "You must now be brave. You are needed greatly. The fate of your children—the fate of us all—lies with you."

Oh, she could not. She wanted to know her sons. She wanted her sons to know her. How could she leave them? How could she die? Surely she could use her reawakened magic to change fate.

But Queen Vivian's heart would not let her hope, for even while her mind did not fully understand what the prophet said, her heart did. If she did not do what he came to tell her she must do, the whole realm would suffer. And this was something her heart could not accept.

"And my sons will live?" Queen Vivian whispered into the quiet room.

"Yes," the prophet said. It was hardly more than a breath. "They will live, though I cannot say what happens after that. The rest, I presume, is up to them."

Queen Vivian looked from the child in her arms to the old man, two versions of life lying before her. Her arms tightened around her baby. "Then I shall do it," she said, but the old man was not awake to hear it.

Her maidservant, Tilly, a woman with bright pink lips, small green eyes, and a severe knot of mud-brown hair tied at the base of her neck, burst into the room. She saw the prophet on the floor and gasped.

"Please," Queen Vivian said. "Fetch some help. The old prophet has fallen asleep."

"He has died?" Tilly said.

"No," Queen Vivian said. "I believe he is only asleep. But he will need help from my chambers."

"Yes, Your Highness," Tilly said, and she spun away, back through the door, leaving it gaping open. Queen Vivian looked at the man still stretched out on her floor. He had grown slightly younger. She blinked. The wrinkles faded a bit. They were still there, of course, but they were not etched as deeply. She saw that he was not quite as old as she had, at first, thought.

Or perhaps she was only growing weary.

Queen Vivian leaned her head back on the ornate headboard that decorated the top of her bed. The baby within her moved. She smiled, but it was a very sad smile. She would not even know this baby.

She kissed the boy in her arms on his small, heart-shaped lips. "I shall not be here to watch you become king," she said, placing her son on the bed and stretching out beside him. "But I shall always be with you."

And with that, the queen fell into a sleep so deep she did not even see the prophet, who had grown much younger in his state of unconsciousness, stand to his feet, cast a glance at the queen and infant prince, and walk himself out the door of her chambers, his walking stick softly clicking the floor in front of him.

Plans

Much later, on the evening Ruby's magic built a tower in the woods near Rosehaven, Prince Cole crashes into the clearing where he left Rapunzel in a tower and Ruby in a shaky shelter. His clothes are torn, and his face is streaked with dirt, but he is wearing a triumphant grin that no one is around to see. He looks up at the tower and then at the small shelter. He enters the shelter with the bottle of Rapunzel's tears.

Ruby is just as he left her. He stares at her for a moment, not knowing where he should pour the tears. He decides to anoint her head. She does not stir, so he tries a hand. She still does not stir. He pours the last of the tears on her throat. Ruby coughs and opens her eyes.

"Ruby," he says, and he kneels at her side.

"Prince Cole," she says. She is confused, unable to

grasp why she is in her leaning home, and on the floor, no less.

"You collapsed," Prince Cole says. "I thought it wise to drag you in here."

And with sudden clarity, Ruby remembers. "Rapunzel," she says.

"She is safe," Prince Cole says. "Thanks to you. That is a tower no one will be able to climb." His face falls slightly, his eyes turning to glass.

"There is a way," Ruby says, knowing what he does not say. "You can enter. And I can as well." She stands. Her vision blurs, and she stumbles. Prince Cole steadies her and helps her out of her home and into the woods. She stares at the gray tower, so very tall—as tall as the trees of this forest. "Rapunzel," she calls. "Let down your hair."

Nothing happens for the barest instant. And then Rapunzel's face appears at the one window carved into the tower. Ruby and Prince Cole breathe.

"Rapunzel, let down your hair," Ruby says again. Rapunzel stares at her for some minutes before she realizes what Ruby is trying to do. She smiles and lets down her hair. It falls neatly onto the forest floor, a golden rope of silken hair.

Prince Cole looks at Ruby. "Climb it," she says. "I

shall be right behind you."

It is with great effort that Ruby climbs the thick mass of hair. Prince Cole is finished long before she is, and she cannot see it, but he pulls the hair up along with her. She reaches the top of the tower in much less time than she would have if she had been climbing the entire way herself.

When Prince Cole and Rapunzel help her through the window, the first thing Ruby says is, "Did it hurt you? Our climbing?"

Rapunzel shakes her head. Her eyes are brimming with tears. "I am so glad you are here," she says. She embraces Ruby.

"You are cold," Ruby says. She looks around, but she has left her magical staff on the ground. "I will conjure a blanket when I return to the ground."

"You must remain here," Rapunzel says. "I feel much braver when you are here."

"I will protect your tower," Ruby says. "But you will have need of supplies."

"I will gather supplies," Prince Cole says. "There are plenty in my castle." A shadow crosses his face. "How long do you suppose Rapunzel must remain in this tower?"

Ruby shakes her head. "I do not know," she says.

"Until the danger passes."

"And if it does not ever pass?" Rapunzel says. Ruby knows she is speaking of her healing powers, her gift of immortality, the danger that awaits her with Prince Cole's father and any others who might use her for their gain.

"Then we shall remain here with you," Ruby says. She glances at Prince Cole, whose eyes sadden.

"I will visit when I can," Prince Cole says. "But I shall not be able to remain as Ruby can."

Rapunzel slides to the floor. Prince Cole and Ruby do as well, one on each side of her. Rapunzel takes their hands in each of her own. They stare at the stone wall and think their own thoughts and then exchange light and meaningless banter until the room grows gray.

Prince Cole stands. "Well," he says. "I must gather some supplies and then return to the castle, before my father wonders where I am."

"I am sorry," Ruby says.

Prince Cole kneels before her, takes an old, wrinkled hand in his, and kisses the back of it. "You have saved her life," he says. "There is no reason to be sorry for your noble act." The cold that has dripped into Ruby's stomach begins to thaw. Prince Cole casts a longing glance at Rapunzel and says, "I shall return shortly."

"You will check in on my brother, Cole?" Rapunzel

says.

A shadow of sorrow crosses Prince Cole's face. He drops his head. "Of course," he says.

"And let my parents know that I am well," Rapunzel says.

"Yes," Prince Cole says.

"And bring me news."

"I will."

Rapunzel follows him to the window and lets down her hair. Prince Cole disappears, and it is only Ruby and Rapunzel.

Ruby wishes she would have asked Prince Cole to deliver her staff before he left. She files through all the basic enchantments she remembers learning during the first weeks of magic lessons with Arthur, the Fairendale instructor, and there is one that presents itself to her suddenly and certainly. A Retrieval spell. She performs it, and the staff appears in her hand. She exclaims, and Rapunzel marvels.

Quite by accident, Rapunzel spies a small box resting in the corner of the tower. She holds it out to Ruby, who does not peer inside, only turns it into the most majestic bed either of them has ever seen, complete with three feather mattresses bound together, pale rose-colored curtains that close around it, and a thick white cover that will keep them warm when the cold sneaks in through the glassless window once the sun has set. Rapunzel claps.

"How lovely," she says and stretches out in it. She is so exhausted that she falls immediately to sleep.

Ruby watches her for a time and then turns her attention to the window, which she will guard all night to ensure that no creatures or people enter uninvited, if such a thing is possible.

It is unusual for the Graces to consult their magical looking ball so late. But something has brought them to the ball, all at the same time, without any of them speaking a word to another. And still without a word, Splendor removes the green cloth that covers their looking ball, and Good Cheer places her hands above the ball so that it glows to life.

The ball shows them only Guardia. But it is confusing. There is nothing much happening in Guardia. There is a large, hairy king, pacing the floor of his castle, monologuing to himself. There is a large, somewhat hairy queen, coming down the castle hallway, perhaps to join her king in his throne room. There are large, hairy white creatures—Yetis they have heard them called—guarding every entrance and doorway of the castle.

The Graces look into every corner of the land. Every corner is black with dark magic, as it has always been. But this time the darkness is slightly darker, a bluish black. Only the castle is bright.

"It has grown stronger," Good Cheer says. "We must watch this land closely."

This unexpected look in the looking ball has caused them to forget all about the monster in the woods.

A small pinprick of light glimmers in a corner of Guardia. Golden words emerge and then fade. *I am here*, it says. And then again: *I am here.*

The Graces look at one another. The ball is not usually so confusing. Good Cheer wonders if they extracted too many of their memories, if they have forgotten something vitally important, if they will have to restore some of them. But how can she restore some of them and not all?

"We must travel to Guardia," Mirth says. "We must retrieve whatever it is that calls to us." Splendor nods.

"No," Good Cheer says. "We must continue waiting."

It is not news that sits well with Mirth and Splendor. But they know that Graces do not argue. Somewhere along the way, Good Cheer became their leader—

perhaps because she was the first—and they must, now, respect her wisdom and her decisions.

"Time for sleep," Good Cheer says.

She will not sleep, however. She will consider. She will peruse her book on the lands of the realm in an attempt to know everything she can possibly know about what beckons them to the land of Guardia.

She will plan.

Marion—or as she is called among the villagers of Lincastle: the Evil Queen—watches from outside a window that looks in upon the sitting room of the Graces. She sees the green looking ball. She longs to steal it. A looking ball would be just as valuable as the looking glass she parted with many years ago. It would show her everything she would like to know. But stealing a looking ball from the Graces would be a nearly impossible task.

She peers in through the window, at the dark-skinned Grace who now sits in a chair and pores over a book by candlelight. She tries to make out what book it is. There are maps. Perhaps a book on the lands of the realm? She has one of those. She has never had much use for it. She prefers paging through the Old Man's Great Book, but she grows frustrated with even that one. The book contains secrets, and she cannot unlock those secrets. Perhaps she should join alliances with the Graces. Perhaps they could show her how to use the book, and she, in turn, could grant them access to it. She knows it would be helpful.

Marion was asked to become a Grace, once upon a time, when there was only one. The Old Man had mentioned it as a desirable opportunity. She had answered him rather flippantly: "I prefer to work alone." She should have considered the deal more thoroughly.

The Graces have no use for her now. If they did, they would have employed her long ago, in the days and weeks after she died and rose again for some unknown and entirely mysterious purpose. Marion gazes up at the moon, which is hazy this eve. It hangs from the sky like a shining white ball, low and luminous.

She has never known why she was raised from the dead to live again. Why is she here? Why did the prophet Bregdon, who had saved her from the greedy hands of the Grim Reaper, leave her and never return? What is her purpose? Marion wraps her arms around herself and clears her throat, a sound that is soft and brittle. She returns her gaze to the room beyond the window. The Grace is still bent over the table.

Marion squints, but she cannot see the page that is open. She feels a cold breath crawl down her neck, and in that moment, the Grace lifts her head and looks directly at her. Marion draws back into the shadows, back into anonymity. She hopes she has not been seen, or, worse, recognized.

She touches her staff gently, silently, to the ground, and she disappears in a wisp of black smoke.

Marion possesses the full range of magical powers, though she was a mother, though she died. She is yet another who breaks all the magical rules in our story.

Perhaps it would now be helpful to inform you that those who have been given the full range of sorcery— access to both dark and light magic—are those sorcerers and sorceresses who contain within them the capacity to practice both light and dark magic, as magic determines at birth. Some sorcerers are only given a capacity for light magic, and it is unknown why (dark magic is never gifted without light magic balancing it out). The magic generally decides, though Mages, who have not yet made an appearance in our story and who are the only sorcerers and sorceresses who can awaken magic where it did not exist before, are also permitted to decide.

Both light and dark magic reside in most sorcerers and sorceresses in varying capacities. They can practice light magic for their purposes, or they can turn to dark magic, with great caution. Those with a larger measure of dark and light magic, like Marion, sometimes retain their powers even after passing along magical powers to their children. It is a mysterious thing.

Marion has been exceedingly lonely in her years as the Evil Queen, and this loneliness has manifested itself in a tireless study of the Old Man's Great Book, which contains all the light and dark enchantments available to sorcerers in the realm. In the last several years, Marion has focused nearly exclusively on dark magic. She has excelled at it. In fact, she has accumulated an impressive store of strange enchantments. For example, recently, as she idled away the hours in her small cottage on the other side of these woods, she flattened herself so efficiently that she appeared to be merely a rug in the room. It was a complicated spell, and her hair hung out in golden waves on one side of the rug, an unintentional mistake; the second time she performed the spell, there was no such mistake. (Perfecting, she believes, only takes practice.)

Marion has also transformed herself into a tree and then back into her lovely self, summoned words from her tea kettle and conducted a lengthy conversation with porcelain, and unlocked a door using a flick of the wrist.

It is astounding what one can do with a bit of dark magic.

Upon entering her home, Marion touches the bracelet at her wrist, which unfolds into her staff. She gazes at it. No marks have been added. She had been told, before trapping the Prophet Folen into a magical mirror that now resides in the throne room of Fairendale castle, that her staff would mark how many Black Eyed Beings have been destroyed. There are not many notches. She wishes she had kept Folen's staff, which counted how many Black Eyed Beings were in the Grim Reaper's army.

Perhaps it is time for her to hunt. Perhaps that is her mission, why she has been spared death and was given another life.

She shivers. Even Marion, with all her light and dark magic, does not fancy meeting Black Eyed Beings. She has come upon only one in her life, and that was more than enough. But the Grim Reaper is an ever-present foe for those who have died and lived again. He does not like being cheated.

She will need the looking ball to hunt. It is the only way she will be able to see them. They are, for most, invisible.

Marion crosses the room and approaches a table, on

which sits a thick book bound in brown leather. The Old Man's Great Book. She pages through it. She knows precisely which spell she will use to capture the looking ball and make it hers.

And then she will begin her hunt.

In the shadows, her wicked smile gleams.

There was another who watched outside the cottage of the Graces. He is the one who commanded the attention of the Grace who appeared to look right at Marion, for he stood just behind the Evil Queen. He had almost reached her with his gleaming silver scythe when she vanished into thin air. He gripped his scythe hard enough to crack three bones in his left hand. He stared at them for a moment before he healed them.

Now he looks past the spot where Marion stood, into the window that glows its warm light into the woods. The Grace stands, looking back at him, her eyes wide but unafraid. This angers him immensely. But he smiles, the thin white skin twisting around the corners of his mouth. The Grace lifts her staff. He slips back into the shadows.

These ones who have eluded him, these ones who have cheated death, will pay in the end. He will find his opportunity, and he will not merely recruit them for his army. He will imprison them in his army. He will command them to work a new kind of fate—a much darker one.

First, however, he must procure a copy of the Old Man's Great Book. There are not many in the land. Three, he thinks. One that is hidden, two that are kept inside abodes—a castle and a home—which is a problem for him, since he cannot enter any place, besides forests and open land and streets that run through villages, without being invited. This is, however, a simple technicality that he plans to work around, eventually. When he builds such a vast army that he will be all-powerful. When he gathers enough magic from the dead and dying that he becomes unstoppable.

And when he is unstoppable, he will be able to talk, touch, live. That is all he really wants. To be seen, to be heard, to be touched and felt and known. It is the touch that he misses the most. He rubs a bony arm.

And perhaps when he has had his fill of living again, he will seek a crown. After all, he will live forever. Forever is quite a long time without a kingdom to rule.

The Grim Reaper turns, his black robes flapping around the bones of his ankles. He is still but a shadow. White at the edges and growing more substantial every day, but still only a shadow.

He slices his scythe through a tree, sending it crashing to the forest floor, before disappearing into the beclamored woods.

Fate

It all happened precisely as the prophet foretold. In the days after Jem visited, Queen Vivian marked the enchantment in the instructions he had left in the castle library and practiced chanting it, even singing it to her son, over and over again.

She spent more time with the king, using her influence to soften his features and his heart as well. He looked on her with great love, and it tore at her heart, for she knew that his would break when she died. But she took what little she had and gave what she could. The king remained in her chambers until long into the night, talking with her about the kingdom and their sons. He left her hallways lit, and sometimes he even brought her a small gift. He told her he loved her many times.

It was over too soon, and the time came for birthing

her second child. She died before she even heard his first cry.

The words of the spell had only just left her lips when the darkness surrounded her and she felt herself falling, falling, falling, and then, abruptly, lifted back into light. An old man, shorter and stouter than the one who had told her of her fate, hovered over her as she blinked, trying to orient herself to the world in which she awoke.

"Ah," he said. "I see you are here. Very well, then." He leaned back on his heels and dusted off his robe, blowing a long breath out his mouth. "They almost had you."

She pulled herself up on an elbow, but her head was dizzy. In front of her was the most astonishing sight. Another man floated in the air. He stared at her with eyes that glowed orange. His bluish head was so bare she could see the sun reflecting off of it. He wore large golden bracelets with red and blue jewels affixed to them around the tops of his arms as well as his wrists. His chest, which was a slight bluish color, matching his face, was bare except for a small blue vest ringed in gold. Feathers of jewels hung from his earlobes. He did not say a word, only stared at her contemptuously, as though she had done something wrong.

"Please," the older man said, "Lie back down. Good

Cheer will be here soon. I will remain with you until she arrives."

So Queen Vivian did as she was told and closed her eyes. The world was alive around her, birds singing and squawking and calling to one another in a language she could not understand. She had never heard such noise. It hurt her already-throbbing head.

When she woke again, there were two distinct voices around her: one of a man and one of a woman. She opened her eyes to see a woman with smooth brown skin, dark black hair arranged in braids down her back, and a neck covered in strings of pearls, one row stacked on top of another. She looked like a queen. Queen Vivian sat up again. The old man was there, but the bald, floating one was not. Perhaps she had dreamed that part, then.

"Well," the woman said. "You have woken."

The old man cleared his throat. "This is the one you have waited for, Good Cheer."

Queen Vivian's eyes met those of the woman called Good Cheer. Her eyes were dark and bottomless, but they brightened when she said, "Yes. I will no longer be alone."

The words felt as though they were alive, reaching into Queen Vivian's chest and igniting it in warmth and relief. She would not have to be alone, either.

"Thank you for your work, Bregdon," Good Cheer said. Queen Vivian saw that Good Cheer was speaking to the old man. She had read of a prophet by the same name in one of the castle library books. She had thought—no, she was sure—he was dead.

"Bregdon?" she said.

The prophet turned to her. His eyes softened a bit, and he let out a choppy laugh. "Ah," he said. "I see you know who I am. Perhaps we should explain."

"We must get her to safety," Good Cheer said. "And then we can explain."

Good Cheer and Bregdon lifted Queen Vivian and carried her through the woods and over a small bridge and into a warm and bright cottage. It was plain, unobtrusive, with a curtained stand in a corner; a couple of chairs that appeared to have wings on their backs, very like the chairs in the Fairendale castle library; and a wooden table, around which were four wooden chairs. Good Cheer pulled one out for Queen Vivian and gestured that she sit.

"Now we can talk," Good Cheer said.

Queen Vivian sat, and the other two gathered around her.

"Bregdon," Good Cheer began, "is responsible for creating the Graces."

"Well," Bregdon said. His mop of white hair shook a little. "Not only me. Also the djinn."

"Ah, yes," Good Cheer said. "Kadesh." She spoke the word with contempt.

"He was gracious enough to pull the both of you from death," Bregdon said.

"Because he owed you three wishes," Good Cheer said. "That is the only reason. Do not give Kadesh a kindness he does not possess."

Queen Vivian stared at the two of them. She had only heard stories of djinns. She had never known they were real. Bregdon looked at her and shook his head slightly. "Djinns are magical men holed away in some object," he said. "When they are released, they are bound to give their releasor three wishes."

"And you released a djinn?" Queen Vivian said. "How did you do that?"

Bregdon shrugged. "I found the object, and I released its magic," he said. "Its magic was a djinn."

Queen Vivian closed her eyes and slowly opened them again. She had known this new world to which she had been brought would not be easy to understand.

"Perhaps you have never encountered a djinn," Good Cheer said.

Queen Vivian shook her head. "I have been nowhere

but a castle for most of my life. And before that, the village of Eastermoor."

Good Cheer looked at her and tilted her head. "How very sad," she said. "But we shall remedy that with our work."

"Our work?" Queen Vivian said.

Bregdon held up a hand. "Allow me," he said to Good Cheer. "The djinn I released, yes, owed me three wishes. I used them to bring three of you back to life." His eyes flicked to Good Cheer. She scowled at him.

For a woman named Good Cheer, she did not seem to harbor good cheer. Queen Vivian smiled to herself, but she kept her face somber for now.

"One of them did not work out," Good Cheer said. "Even with the help of a mermaid." She sighed. "So, for now, there is only you and me."

"And what are we?" Queen Vivian said.

"The Graces," Bregdon said.

Queen Vivian turned her full attention upon the prophet now. "I read in a book that you were dead," she said. "How do you sit before me now?"

Bregdon's eyes lit up as though he was amused. He clapped his hands once. "A well read one," he said, and he gave Good Cheer a significant look. Then he leaned forward across the table. His eyes danced. "I, too, was brought back from the brink of death." He leaned back again. "For the purpose of creating you." His voice lifted at the end of it, his mirth spilling out.

"Who brought you back to life?" Queen Vivian said.

Bregdon waved a small hand with crooked fingers. "That matters not," he said. "Only that I am here, now."

"You are the oldest of the prophets," Queen Vivian said.

"I am," Bregdon said.

"It is impossible that you are still alive," Queen Vivian said.

"Yes, quite," Bregdon said. His eyes danced.

They were quiet for a moment, and then Queen Vivian said, "Where is the djinn now?"

"He is free," Bregdon said, his smile so giddy it was nearly contagious. Queen Vivian liked him very much.

"Free to terrorize the land," Good Cheer said.

"I do not believe that is who Kadesh is," Bregdon said.

"You always did believe too kindly of others," Good Cheer said.

Queen Vivian could see that they had known each other for quite some time, though Good Cheer had not a line on her face.

Good Cheer rose from her place at the table. She

spread out her arms so the wide, gaping sleeves of her white robe shimmered, and the green of her dress shone through in places. "Welcome to the sisterhood," she said. And for the first time, she smiled. "You shall be called Splendor." She reached for a staff that leaned against a cast iron stove and pointed it toward Queen Vivian. The old gown Queen Vivian had worn for the birthing of her son faded, and in its place was a lovely gown of green with golden flourishes twirling across the silken threads.

"Splendor," Queen Vivian said, trying out the new name.

"Splendor," Good Cheer said. "And now we wait for Mirth."

"In this cottage," Queen Vivian said.

"Yes," Good Cheer said. "Your new home, in the kingdom of Lincastle."

"And what of my family?" Queen Vivian said.

"You must move on," Bregdon said. "Forget them. You are now a Protector of the realm."

"But might I check in with them? Might I see the new babe?" Queen Vivian's voice broke with a longing that was too terrible to bear.

"It will only cause you more pain," Bregdon said, and he turned away.

But Good Cheer put a hand on Queen Vivian's

shoulder. "Come," she said. "I will show you in my looking ball."

At that, Bregdon turned around again. "I do not consider that a good idea," he said, but Good Cheer gave him a withering look.

"At times," she said, "it is good for closure to look in on the ones we have left behind."

"You are only permitted one look," Bregdon said.

"We are permitted more," Good Cheer whispered so that Bregdon could not hear. "The prophet does not know it. And I do not tell." The words seemed to indicate that Good Cheer had family she looked in on as well. The thought spread warmth into Queen Vivian's chest. Good Cheer continued: "When our circle is complete, our memories will fade. We can remember and observe while we are permitted. The prophet would not agree, but, well, he has never been a mother." She smiled at Queen Vivian.

Good Cheer took her to a tall stand in the corner of the room, which was draped with a bit of green cloth. Iron claws reached up and curled toward nothing. Good Cheer's hands hovered over the stand, and a looking ball appeared, glowing green.

Queen Vivian gasped. She had never seen a looking ball. It was quite beautiful.

"Now," Good Cheer said. "You must look without emotion. It is emotion that makes our looking dangerous. Rid yourself of it."

Queen Vivian did not know how she could do that, but she closed her eyes tightly and tried to remember that now she was no longer Queen Vivian but Splendor. She had no family ties. She was merely looking in a ball to ensure that a royal family was alive and well.

The sound of a squalling baby pulled her eyes back open. The baby was small and red-faced, with rolls around his middle and down his legs. He looked healthy and strong. Angry as well. Tears crept down her face, as hard as she tried to withhold them.

In a corner of the room, King Sebastien was crying. His hands covered his face. He was saying something that sounded like "My queen, my queen," over and over again. The tears grew thicker on Queen Vivian's face.

What would her death do to him? She could not bear to consider it. She could not bear, either, to look away.

King Sebastien, as she watched, stood up. A shadow crossed his face. He ordered out everyone but the nurse who had cared for Prince Wendell while Queen Vivian slept. "From now on," the king told the nurse when all the others had left the room, "you will keep the birth of both my children silent. They shall be known as twins.

Their mother died in the year after birthing twins, do you understand?" His voice had picked up desperation and flung it across the many miles to where Queen Vivian stood in a cottage, watching him. She shook with sadness.

The nurse in the glass nodded, a bewildered look on her face. Queen Vivian felt the uncertainty, too, though she had been the one to suggest the ruse. How would the kingdom believe such a tale?

The king's eyes hardened into something unrecognizable and rather frightening. In the worst of his days, Queen Vivian had never seen anything like this. "Keep them in their rooms until it is impossible to tell which one is older," he said. "I shall see them then."

"No," Queen Vivian said. He could not keep them in their rooms. Children must run and play. She reached for the glass, but the glass went dark.

"And now you know," Good Cheer said. "There is work we must do."

Queen Vivian hung her head. "He is the one," she said, her voice brittle and hoarse.

"The one?" Good Cheer said.

"The one who will damage the realm," Queen Vivian said. "Perhaps destroy it."

"No," Bregdon said from across the room. "Your

husband will do much, but your son will do even more."

"No," Queen Vivian said. Her voice rose and twisted on the air that whispered through an open window. "He will be a kind ruler. Another prophet told me as much."

"Perhaps the first one would have," Bregdon said. "But it is the second one who will rule the throne. And he will do much harm."

Queen Vivian's legs buckled, but Good Cheer caught her. "Do not worry, Splendor," she said. "You are here to change fate."

"If I were there, I could stop it," Queen Vivian said.

"It is too late for that," Good Cheer said.

"I was tricked," Queen Vivian said. "I would not have taken this, I would not have agreed to it if I had known. I was tricked." She looked around, wildly, for Bregdon, but Good Cheer, at that very moment, touched her staff to Queen Vivian's cheek. Queen Vivian felt her body grow soft. Good Cheer carried her into a room with a green covering on its bed and laid her in it, drawing the blanket up to her chin. She sat in a chair beside the bed.

While Queen Vivian rested, Good Cheer told her about the family she had left so many years ago. She told Queen Vivian that what they were doing was much bigger than family. Queen Vivian had no questions, for she could hardly think. At least until Good Cheer said,

"And now we must wait."

"For what?" Queen Vivian said, her voice echoing in her ears as though it were hollow.

"Not for what. For whom," Good Cheer said. "We wait for our third sister. And then our work shall begin in earnest."

In the days and weeks and months after, Queen Vivian and Good Cheer shared a table and a home and even small tasks to shift fate here and there. They became a family of their own, and little by little, as the years passed on, Queen Vivian became Splendor.

And across the miles, a king's heart broke and healed again, twisted.

Explanations

Prince Cole does not return to the tower before mid-afternoon the following day. He is laden with a basket of books, a basket of food, and another basket with blankets and pillows. "I have brought supplies," he calls from the ground. "Rapunzel, let down your hair."

Rapunzel throws her golden hair out the window and leans over the sill. "How will you carry all of that up here?" she says.

Prince Cole hooks the handles of the baskets around his elbows—two on one arm and one on another. "I shall manage," he says, and Rapunzel laughs. Ruby watches.

Prince Cole begins to climb, but before he is halfway to the top, movement at the corner of the woods catches Ruby's eye.

"They are here," she says, and it is true. The men fan

out in the clearing, their weapons drawn. Swords, bows, and some gleaming daggers.

Prince Cole, by now, has pulled himself into the tower. He looks back out the window with a scowl on his face. "Well," he says. He drops the baskets in the small stone room. "I will see to this."

"And I with you," Ruby says. She turns to Rapunzel. "As soon as we slide back down your hair, you must immediately pull it up. And do not let it down for anyone, no matter what they say. No matter what they do."

Rapunzel's tears begin to fall. "But you cannot leave me," she says.

"It is for your safety and protection," Ruby says. She pulls Rapunzel close to her and closes her eyes, breathing in the strong scent of chamomile. It fortifies her.

When Ruby lets go of Rapunzel, they are both crying. But Ruby does not say another word. Prince Cole slides down Rapunzel's hair first, followed by a terrified Ruby. She never did like daring acts like sliding down a silken rope from such a height.

A man has crossed the clearing, clearly intent on snatching the golden rope that is shortening rapidly, but Prince Cole barrels into him. The man makes an "Ooomf" sound, and Ruby stills, her staff clutched tightly in her right hand.

"Keep your distance," Prince Cole warns the other men. The man with whom he collided has already pulled himself to his feet, his sword held straight in front of him, its blade mere inches from Prince Cole's chest.

"Let us in that tower," he growls. "We will have the girl."

"She is no lost child of Fairendale," Prince Cole says. "And you will not have her."

"You will have me," Ruby says. "I am a lost child of Fairendale."

Ruby can feel Prince Cole's eyes on her. The men blink at her. And then they laugh. It is some minutes before the leader of their group, the man with a sword pointed at Prince Cole, speaks. "You are an old woman."

"Under a spell," Ruby says. "Return me, and the king of Fairendale will reward you handsomely."

The man ignores her. "Let us in that tower," he says.

"Never," Prince Cole says. He turns authoritatively to the other men—eleven of them gathered in a semi-circle. "As your future king, I command you to let the girl go."

"You are not king yet," says the man in front of him. "And perhaps you will never be."

Prince Cole takes a step back, and in that moment, the man lurches, grabs Ruby, and slides the blade to her throat. Prince Cole lifts his hands.

"Do not do this, Max," Prince Cole says. Ruby does not move.

"I will kill this woman if you do not let us in the tower."

"Do not let them," Ruby says with a calm she cannot explain. "I am prepared to die." This angers the man, and he presses the blade closer to her throat, but still she does not fight him. "Listen, Prince Cole," she says instead. "I have lost practically everything. I do not know if there is anything left for me in Fairendale. My father, my best friend, my home—they are likely all gone. I am prepared to die so that you and Rapunzel might live."

Prince Cole's eyes turn to glass. "No," he whispers.

But at that moment their attention is turned elsewhere, to a corner of the clearing where a Huntsman has stepped out from the shadows, bow drawn. Beside him is a beautiful woman with fiery hair that lifts and twirls in the wind. She looks at them all in turn, her sharp green eyes like emeralds in her pale face. Ruby has seen this woman before. She is the Enchantress who took Hazel and gave Maude and the lost children of Fairendale a shoe-shaped house.

The men shift uneasily. The Enchantress lifts a lovely hand. "We do not come for you," she says in a mellifluous voice. The Huntsman keeps his arrow pointed directly at the man whose blade is pressed against Ruby's throat. "We only come for the girl, and then we shall be out of your way."

The Enchantress taps her staff once against the ground.

Prince Cole lunges for Ruby, seizing his moment, but she is no longer there. He stares at the place where she was, his mouth shocked into opening. A blackbird soars past him and lands on the uplifted finger of the woman in green.

The Enchantress smiles at the people. She lifts a black iron cage and deposits the blackbird inside. Only then does she speak.

"The girl in the tower is not one of the magical children for whom the king of Fairendale searches," she says. "And because you have threatened to take her life, because you would use her for your own selfish purposes, you will never reach her again." She waves her staff toward the tower and a rustling noise fills the clearing. Brambles grow at an alarming rate, a whole thicket of green thorns forming before their eyes. The brambles continue crawling, all the way up to the top of the tower. And when they have finished growing, the tower and the brambles vanish.

The Enchantress spreads her hands before the men who gather in the clearing. Every eye is fixed on her, including those of the Huntsman.

"My dear men of Rosehaven," she says. "Go back to your homes."

"Give us the girl," a man shouts. "We would have her reward."

The eyes of the Enchantress widen and then narrow. The green flickers with fury. "As I have already said, she is not a child of Fairendale. She is a child of your own village."

"It makes no matter," another man says. "We have need of that reward. It is worth the sacrifice."

The Enchantress studies them for some moments. No one dares to move. She takes her time looking at each of the men, while the Huntsman thinks of the irony—that a child of Fairendale stood before their noses and yet they did not believe her. "Your greed," the Enchantress says, "will be your downfall." And then she thumps her staff on the ground, says some words, and closes her eyes. The men vanish, carried on a wind back to the village of Rosehaven, where they will be deposited into their beds, unable to rise for at least the remainder of the day.

The Enchantress looks at the cage in her hand and back at the boy in the middle of the clearing. Her eyes lift to the invisible tower.

The Huntsman watches her in wonder.

She turns to the boy. "Go on home. Your friend will be safe."

"But how will I find her?" the boy says.

"You will not," the Enchantress says. "Until the time is right."

The boy looks at her for a moment. He appears to reconsider all the questions he would like to ask and instead runs back toward Rosehaven. The Enchantress turns her eyes to the Huntsman. "Let us go."

"No one will find the tower?" he says. "The girl will be safe?"

"No one will find it," the Enchantress says, and then her body tilts, as though the world has shifted on its axis, and the Huntsman must lunge to keep her on her feet. He draws her back into shadows.

She is much weaker than she lets on. She is expending too much magic. She must rest. Magic does not come in unlimited supply; it always has a price.

He does not want to tire her further, but there is something that burns his tongue. He must ask. And so he says, "Will the girl be able to come and go as she wishes?

Or is she a prisoner?"

The Enchantress turns on him in a gust of anger. "You think I would make an unnecessary prisoner out of an innocent girl?" she says.

The Huntsman drops his eyes.

"It was the old crone—the lost girl—who made her a prisoner," the Enchantress says. She holds up the blackbird captured in the iron cage. "I have undone what I could. The girl in the tower will have food and water and everything her heart desires. But she will not leave the tower until it is discovered, until the purest heart can rescue her from it—or until she can rescue herself." She peers into the cage at the blackbird.

The bird twitters. The other birds, lined up in the cart, begin to twitter as well. It is a singing of sorts, but the Enchantress waves her hand and silences them. "They are a nuisance," she says. "I should have known. I should have chosen any creature but a blackbird."

The Huntsman does not say aloud what crosses his mind. Did she choose blackbird, or did the magic choose for her? She seems uncomfortable with the magnitude of her gift, still. He knows she has not had it in its current form for long. She had the gift of magic, but a slightly weaker sort. Magic is not kind to those who lack in skill, as can be seen by the girl locked in a tower, a prisoner of good intentions.

"What about the king's reward?" the Huntsman says. "It might put us in a difficult spot in the other kingdoms, as it did with these men."

"Men are nothing to magic," the Enchantress says. She takes a step toward the cart, presumably to place yet another cage beside the others. Her steps falter, and the Huntsman steadies her again.

"You are more tired than you should be," he says. "You must not use more magic than necessary."

The Enchantress waves him away. "Do not concern yourself with the reward," she says, seeming to ignore his entreaty. "We will find the remaining lost children, and the people will be persuaded, in one way or another, to hand them over to us."

He does not know how she can be so confident. Suppose the news of their coming spreads throughout the kingdoms and the people are ready for them when they enter the lands? Will they not stand out, a Huntsman and an Enchantress—one looking like a walking tree and the other like a beautiful woman?

The Enchantress turns on her heel and tilts her head. "What I do not quite understand is why the king issued a reward at all," she says. "He has sent us to find the children. Why would he need more?"

"The king is not a patient man," the Huntsman says. "We have been traveling for more than a fortnight. Perhaps he believes we will not return."

"Perhaps we should send word, then," the Enchantress says. "Perhaps we should tell him that extending this reward will interfere with our delicate work. It will surely reach the ears of the lost children. And if we are unable to find them all..." She stares past him, as though lost in another realm of possibility.

"And how would we send word from the middle of a forest?" the Huntsman says.

The eyes of the Enchantress focus on his face once again. The corner of her mouth turns up. "Have you never heard of using ravens to carry important messages?"

He has, of course. The Huntsman is a well-read man. It is only that he has seen no ravens. He has not seen many birds in this forest at all.

"You have seen ravens in this forest?" he says.

"No," she says, turning back to the cart. She places the newly captured blackbird within it. "But that does not mean I cannot find one."

The Huntsman smiles. He admires her persistence, her ingenuity, her poise.

The Enchantress stares at the line of cages.

Something seems to occur to her, and she turns to look at the Huntsman. "Well then," she says. "We shall know soon enough where we will travel next. But perhaps we might give the looking ball some time to…" A pause. A glance down at her shoe. "Gather the information while we celebrate our latest success with a jaunt into town."

"But they will recognize us," the Huntsman says.

The Enchantress smiles widely at him now. "Rest assured, Huntsman. We will not see any of the men who entered this clearing. I regret to say they have taken to their beds and cannot rise until morning. Would you care to eat in a tavern this eve?"

The Huntsman's stomach grumbles in reply. He laughs. "That would be lovely," he says.

The Enchantress turns back to the blackbirds momentarily. She waves her staff over them and whispers some words the Huntsman cannot hear. When she faces him again, she is beaming. "A Concealment spell should keep them safe enough," she says.

The Huntsman looks past her shoulder. "But I can still see them," he says.

"As you should," the Enchantress says. "The horse, the cart, and the captured blackbirds can only be seen by you and me." She strides past the Huntsman, though slowly and carefully, as if she might be afraid of stumbling. She is still weary. But food will strengthen her. Or so the Huntsman tells himself.

The gates that bar entry to the village are closed and bolted, but the Enchantress flicks a wrist, and they open. The stone wall around the village shakes only slightly.

The people do not pay them much mind, though they must be an unusual pair by anyone's standards. The people strut about the town as though they can see nothing but the path they are taking. The Enchantress and the Huntsman watch the scene for a time, their eyes caught most by the beggars in the streets, who do not gain even a moment of attention from the people who stride past them.

In the tavern, they hear many things. They hear about the men who plan to round up every child of Rosehaven, for the sake of payment. They hear about a certain group of parents in the village, who keep their children safe and indoors so that they are not captured unaware. They hear about the reward King Willis offers.

"There is much unrest in this land," the Huntsman says when they have finished their supper—bread for the both of them, lamb and buttered greens for the Huntsman, and, for the Enchantress, a bowl of soup so thick with vegetables it could hardly be called soup.

"I daresay we will find unrest wherever we travel

now," the Enchantress says. "It seems the king has not made this quest any easier for us."

"Did we expect him to?" the Huntsman says.

The Enchantress shakes her head. "I expected worse," she says.

A scuffle sounds in the doorway of the tavern. A man is there, a man who walks with a bed bending his back. It is comical to see, and the people in the tavern shout and point and laugh. The face of the man who carries the bed on his back turns crimson—nearly purple. He searches the tavern. His eyes fasten on the Huntsman.

"Trouble," the Huntsman murmurs, before he stands to his feet. He did not bring his sword. He will have to use his hands for this brawl.

"You," the man says, and he levels a finger at the back of the Enchantress. Her eyes narrow, and she stands slowly and just as slowly turns around to look at the man.

"Well," she says. "I see I should have used stronger magic."

The man struggles to pull the bed attached to his back through the door of the tavern and, after several moments of ducking, turning, and rearranging, he remains in the doorway. He addresses those gathered in the tavern.

"She turned an old crone into a blackbird," he says.

"She made one of our children vanish into thin air." He glares at the Enchantress. "Our children are not safe with that…that…creature here."

The people turn their eyes to the Enchantress. "She did not vanish," the Enchantress says. "She is simply… concealed."

Murmurs of "sorceress" begin to thread through the tavern's people, who have also risen to their feet. The Huntsman glances around. They are backed into a corner, as though this trap was preordained. He shoves that thought away, however.

"Perhaps you come from a land that welcomes sorcerers and sorceresses," says the man. "But in this land…" His eyes take on a menacing look. "They are burned at the stake."

No one moves.

"Come along, Huntsman," the Enchantress says. "I see we are not welcome here."

Someone spits in their direction. The Enchantress pauses and holds up her hand. The room stills, as though everyone holds a collective breath. The Huntsman watches her hand, on which a ring turns of its own accord.

So she has brought her staff. His heart rises into his throat.

The Enchantress drops her hand and begins to move, weaving through the people, but when they have nearly reached the door, one of the men, who was not in the clearing and does not recognize their faces, grips the wrist of the Huntsman.

The Enchantress stops abruptly and tilts her head before turning around. "Unhand him," she says. "You do not want to know what we can do." The man takes a step back, the Huntsman stumbling with him. The Enchantress flicks her wrist, and everyone winces. Her eyes flash. "I said unhand him," she says in a softer yet more terrifying voice. When the man does not heed her words, she shakes her head. "Well. You leave me no choice then."

The ring on her finger bursts into a staff. She turns in a slow circle. "Your children are not safe with you here," she says. "You would sell them for more money? You would grow richer off those who love you? Tell me, what kind of protection is that?" She shakes her head and answers for them. "It is no protection at all." She slams her staff to the ground, and her lips move as though she is speaking, though her words cannot be heard.

The people shift. "What are you doing?" a woman says.

The Enchantress lifts her chin. "It is already done,"

she says.

"What is done?" the woman says.

"Your children are safe," the Enchantress says. "From you." She looks at the Huntsman and gestures toward the door. "Shall we leave them to their empty, miserable lives?"

The Huntsman follows her out the door. Once they have cleared it, they run, the Enchantress using her magic to speed them along. When they are safe inside the woods, the Huntsman says, "Tell me, what did you do?"

The Enchantress smiles to herself. "I protected the children from those who would sell them," she says.

"But how?" he says.

"By transferring them to the homes where they will be safe," the Enchantress says.

"But they will return to their own homes," the Huntsman says.

"Perhaps," the Enchantress says. "Yes. If their mothers and fathers have a change of heart, if they will protect rather than sell. If they will give their children a future." The Enchantress turns her blazing eyes to his. "Then they shall be returned."

The Huntsman does not say anything. He does not have a chance, for the Enchantress crumples before him. He drops to her side. "What is it?" he says.

Her voice is a papery whisper. "I am only weary," she says. "I must rest."

The Huntsman looks around. "Not here," he says, and he lifts her in his arms and carries her to the clearing, where the horse and cart and the five blackbirds in cages await their return. There is nothing on which to lay her but the cart with the blackbirds. He shrugs off his coat of many colors and places it across her form. And then he sits at her feet and waits.

The words of Queen Clarion circle round and round and round in the king's head.

Let the children go.

Our beautiful land is dying.

I am sorry.

The last and final words mar him the most. When she said them, she had looked as she used to, back when she was a girl, back when she had pleaded with his father to show him, Willis, mercy, and his father had refused. Queen Clarion had looked at him the way she used to look at his father.

I'm sorry, her eyes had said then.

I'm sorry, her eyes said tonight.

He has become his father, or something close to it. Was he as cruel as King Sebastien had been? How had he become this monster? He was not always this way, was he?

King Willis covers his face with his large hands. He heaves in a breath and heaves it back out, unaware that his eyes have filled and spilled and wet the collar of his cape.

How could he allow this most beautiful of all lands to lose its color and its sunlight and its children? How had he not noticed what sort of land it had become without its children? How could he do this to his people?

He had loved them once, had he not? He remembers. The memories, these last several hours that have stretched into a day, have come in flashes, uncurling from a space in his mind he did not know existed. There is a memory here now, one that involves Sir Greyson, an old woman, and a bottle of medicine. The heart of the king aches, a wrenching that causes him to cry out. He remembers the day he saw Sir Greyson caring for his mother. King Willis had wept for his own mother, wept for this love he had never known.

Another flash brings the face of his father, and King Willis shakes his head roughly, violently, to pull a curtain over that memory. Can a king cover one memory without covering all the rest? Another flash, and there is a golden-haired child and a red-haired child, running through the streets of Fairendale, laughing—one a future queen and one his intended princess. He remembers smiling at their cupped hands over ears as they whispered to one another and looked at the two brothers who stood watch. Another flash, and there is his brother, smiling at him, handing him a piece of parchment with their coded language of symbols and shapes. *There is no greater brother in all the lands than you*, the message had said, and beneath it, *I love you.*

The pictures exist in his memory. It is only that he has not seen them for some time. How did he forget them all? How did he forget who he had been years ago? He pulls his hands from his face and straightens. He does not remember walking through the door of the throne room, but here he is. Something hums. He should not have come. He tries to turn but finds that his feet do not work. Something draws him forward in a jerking motion, and he is powerless to stop his steps.

"No," he says to his legs. "Do not go."

But his legs, alas, do not listen.

"No," King Willis says. "I must remember. I cannot forget again."

But his mind, dear reader, does not listen either. He does not see the violet-hued cloud barreling toward him, but he feels when it collides with his chest. It is cold and then warm and then…nothing.

There is a hand, however. The hand of a boy, a boy who is always watching. This boy's hand reaches out for his king and yanks him backward. This boy's hand tightens its grip when something that feels like a wind rips through the throne room and beats them both back. This boy's hand wins, and both the boy and the king stumble out the throne room doors, safe if only for a moment.

The cloud dissipates, as if it did not even exist.

"Sire," Garth says. His legs wobble, but he manages to keep himself and the king on their feet. "I beg you not to go back in there."

"No," King Willis says. "No, 1 must remember."

"The throne room will not allow you to remember," Garth says. "It means for you to forget. The throne and the mirror…"

King Willis stares at the boy. Who is he? How does he know about the throne and the mirror?

The king, momentarily overcome with panic, shoves the boy from him and takes off as fast as he can go—which is not very fast at all—toward the bedchambers of his queen.

He bursts inside without a knock.

Queen Clarion is staring at a wall, holding a crooked

red-brown staff. She thrusts the staff from her hands, and it becomes a red-brown chair. He has sat in that chair before. He looks from it to her and back again.

"May I?" he says, deciding it is not yet time to ask about this chair. He gestures toward it, asking for permission rather than explanation.

Queen Clarion does not say anything. He sits.

"You have bidden me remember," he says. "And I have remembered."

Her face brightens. "You have remembered?"

"I was a good man once," King Willis says. "What happened to me?"

"Your father happened to you," Queen Clarion says. She sits on the end of her bed, which is beautifully made with rich red coverings. The walls, though King Willis does not notice this right now, contain elaborate paintings of the Violet Sea in various forms and circumstances. Queen Clarion, long before this day in which the king and queen sit and frankly speak in her bedchambers, commissioned the village artist to paint these walls, for she has never quite been able to break free of her curiosity—in some worlds, it might be called an obsession—about the waters stories say no man has ever crossed.

"And what else?" King Willis says. "You spoke of an evil influence."

"Yes," Queen Clarion says. Her voice is more whisper than substance. "The throne and the mirror, I believe, are cursed."

"My father is in the mirror," King Willis says. "He wants something."

Queen Clarion does not appear surprised in the least. "What does he want?"

"I believe he would like to rule the kingdom again," King Willis says. "I believe he means to escape the mirror's hold."

Queen Clarion shudders, her eyes searching the waters of her walls. She shifts her gaze back to his. "Then I suppose we must ensure that cannot happen." She stands and walks to one end of her room, which is quite large, and then to the other. When she reaches the far end, she widens the empty hole in King Willis's heart. But when she returns, she fills it in again. Again and again she does this with only a walk from and to him, until he stands and paces with her, so as never to feel the aching absence again.

"Do you know how to prevent this?" King Willis says. "Do you even know how it was done in the first place?"

Queen Clarion stops for a moment, but King Willis continues. He is three feet in front of her before he realizes she is no longer beside him. He turns.

"No," she says. "But perhaps we can find someone who might know." Her eyes cloud, becoming a deep, midnight blue. Then they clear again, a midday sky as it used to look before the world turned gray. "There is a woman in the village."

"The red-haired woman," King Willis says.

Queen Clarion's startled gaze meets his. Her face cracks into a smile. "You do remember," she says.

"I do remember," he says, and they are such light and hopeful and wonderful words that he feels like dancing with them on the air. But instead he says them again, softer. "I do remember."

"You must not return to the throne room," Queen Clarion says.

King Willis drops his gaze. "But what is a king without his throne?"

"A king does not need a throne to rule," Queen Clarion says, and she crosses the short distance to his side. She places a hand on his arm. "A king only needs a purpose."

"We must let the children go," King Willis says.

"Oh, Willis," Queen Clarion says, and she falls into his arms. "How I have longed to hear you say these words. Our son—" But she does not finish, and King Willis knows she cannot, for he feels the tight squeeze of a burning fire in his own throat, all air and words and possibility consumed in its blaze.

He holds her until the moment subsides, and then he says, "There is no time to waste. I must go straightaway."

"Go," Queen Clarion says. "Find the boy in the kitchen. He has been feeding the prisoners. I shall join you shortly."

And King Willis flies—or moves as quickly as he can —out the door. He crosses the long hallway once more, and then he stops, right at the hallway juncture. One way would lead him to the entrance of the castle, where he might visit his people and let them know his new, improved plans. Behind him, he could travel back to the bedchambers and listen to more wisdom from his wife. Another hallway will move him past the throne room and into the kitchen, where Queen Clarion says there is a boy who knows where the door to the dungeons beneath the dungeons is. But King Willis is momentarily struck by such a strong sense of unease and confusion that he does not know which way to go. Where was he going?

He stands, unmoving.

And as he stands, a violet mist gathers at his feet. It is the throne's violet mist. It has broken the barrier between the throne room and here, a junction. King Willis does not notice the mist. It is pale and practically invisible. It has learned from the mistakes of the mirror. King Willis looks toward the castle doors, pointing toward the village, where the people wait for his news. He looks toward the kitchen, where he might find the boy who has fed the prisoners. He looks back toward the long line of bedchambers from which he has come. But, alas, he does not look at his feet.

And while he is not looking at his feet, the violet mist circles, spirals, twists around his toes and his ankles and his legs and his waist and his arms. King Willis finally notices a slight violet glow in the hallway and looks down at himself with horror. The violet mist covers his belly, and even as he watches, a tendril of it pulls back, shapes itself into the triangular head of a terrifying snake, and this time, rather than take a chance on the fickle mind, it strikes straight, puncturing his heart.

King Willis sucks in a breath, and by the time he has released it again, his eyes have turned nearly as black as those of a Black Eyed Being.

The sound of Queen Clarion's footsteps down the hall echo in the silence.

Don't miss the next Fairendale adventure!

Find out what happens when a boy meets a princess who longs
to fly in Book 12: *The Boy Who Loved a Swan.*

An Interview with Ruby

Transcribed by L.R. Patton
Author

L.R.: What was it like waking up in a brand new place?

Ruby: I had expected something like that to happen.

L.R.: You knew about the effects of the Vanishing spell.

Ruby: Yes.

L.R.: What was the first thing you did, upon waking?

Ruby: I made a house. Or, at least, a shelter. I do not think it quite counted as a house. [Laugh]

L.R.: Because of the door?

Ruby: That door. I tried very hard. My magic was wobbly.

L.R.: Wobbly. That is a fantastic description. Tell me more about that.

Ruby: I think when one has been through a Vanishing spell, everything about the person is wobbly. Especially her magic.

L.R.: So you found it difficult to perform your magic.

Ruby: For at least the first bit.

L.R.: But you used your magic to help you make an impressive herb garden.

Ruby: After a few days, yes. For the first few days, I merely gathered water from a nearby tributary and hoped that my father had taught me everything I needed to know about the plants of the forest.

L.R.: The plants you could eat?

Ruby: The plants I could eat and the ones I could not. Not all wild plants can be eaten. Some of them are quite dangerous if consumed.

L.R.: And why did you make a garden?

Ruby: I have always helped with the village gardens in Fairendale. I hated weeding, and that was something my magic did: it weeded my garden so I did not have to. My father never allowed that in Fairendale.

L.R.: What did you grow in your garden?

Ruby: Oh, all sorts of things. Sage, chamomile, peppermint in my herb garden. Some tomatoes and cucumbers in my regular garden.

L.R.: And where did you get seeds?

Ruby: Magic does not need seeds.

L.R.: Right. Well, you certainly seem the most prepared of all the children I have met. To survive in the woods, I mean.

Ruby: My father was a bit of a survivalist. He taught me many things about surviving. I think he did not put much faith in my magic to help me if I were ever in danger.

L.R.: And did you?

Ruby: Well, I do not think it wise to put too much faith in one thing. So I listened to him well.

L.R.: You are a remarkable child, then.

Ruby: My father is a remarkable man.

L.R.: And so are you reunited with him now that you have escaped the Enchantress and the Huntsman?

Ruby: I regret that I cannot say.

L.R.: Well, perhaps I can make my own assumptions. You are no longer a bird.

Ruby: Am I not?

L.R.: You are talking to me.

Ruby: Perhaps I am a talking bird.

L.R.: That is quite ridiculous.

Ruby: I believe our time has come to an end.

L.R.: But I am not finished.

Ruby: It appears that someone else is. Oh, dear.

L.R.: Ruby?

Ruby: It is so dark.

L.R.: Ruby? Where are you?

Ruby:

L.R.: Ruby?

Ruby:

L.R.: This is a most inconvenient end to things. Ruby did give us some clues, however: it is very dark; and someone else is orchestrating the time I am permitted to ask my questions. Perhaps one of the other children I interview will be able to give us additional clues and we might use our excellent powers of deduction to figure out what has become of the Fairendale children. For now, I must leave you with this most unsatisfactory ending.

If you would like to read more Fairendale extras like this, be sure to visit www.lrpatton.com/fairendale.

How to Keep a Secret

By Theo of Fairendale
Secret Sorcerer

Secrets are strange, mysterious things. It is unclear why people keep them, other than that, sometimes, they can seem useful. They hardly ever are, in the end.

I have been carrying a secret for quite some time. I kept my secret because it was necessary. You see, in the land of Fairendale, people do not look kindly on boys who are born with the gift of magic. They look suspiciously on them; they believe that all boys with magic want to steal the sacred throne of Fairendale, since magic is the one requirement for ruling this throne.

I can say, with all honesty, that I have never wanted to steal a throne. But no one would believe me.

It has been quite difficult to keep my magic a secret all my life.

People have all sorts of ways to keep secrets from one another. To keep a secret, one has only to:

Ignore the secret.

Pretend the secret does not exist. Write it out of its existence. Rearrange your world to include all things but the secret.

The problem with this method is that, after a time, the secret will begin gnawing at you, and you will not be able to go anywhere without thinking about it. And it will grow and grow and grow in your mind, like a festering sore, so deep and wide you will not be able to extract it from your heart and mind. It will overtake you until there is only one thing left to do: tell it.

Avoid the person who would be most affected by your secret.

In my case, the person who would be most affected by my secret was Prince Virgil. He was my best friend, along with August, one of the village boys whom I left in the woods near Lincastle. Prince Virgil would, every day, walk from the castle to the village to visit me, Mercy, and Hazel. Therefore, it was practically impossible to avoid Prince Virgil without appearing rude and mean. I am not a rude or mean person, and this method of secret-keeping simply did not work for me, though I was relieved on the days when Prince Virgil did not come into the village and remained, instead, at the castle, where I did not have to think about this secret I was keeping.

When you avoid people, they will always know.

Rewrite your version of the truth in your mind.

This is a dangerous method of secret-keeping that should never be practiced in the mind of a person who would like to keep all their memories. If you rewrite one of your memories, you can be assured that most of your other memories will beg to be rewritten as well, and once this slippery slope begins it is not long before you will wonder what is real and what was simply your own imagination.

Blurt out your secret and pretend you were only in jest.

This method of secret-keeping will only work if you are extremely good at a thing called acting, which is the same as pretending you mean "no" when you say "no." For example, I could have tried the following dialogue with Prince Virgil:

Me: I have the gift of magic.

Prince Virgil: What?

Me: [Very loud laugh]

Prince Virgil: You have the gift of magic?

Mc: No.

Unfortunately (or fortunately, however you want to look at it), I am not very good at acting. I never tried this dialogue, because I knew Prince Virgil would be able to see right through my answer.

Tell the truth.

I know this is not a method of secret-keeping, but it is the best method of secret-elimination. When you have a secret, it is best to simply get it out in the open, clear the air, say what needs saying. Secrets cause unnecessary problems. They are monstrous walls; they will grow while you are sleeping and drive a large, thick wedge between you and the person you love—your mother, your father, your brother, your sister, your best friend.

Telling the truth, revealing your secrets, is the best way to strengthen a relationship, rather than contribute to its crumbling.

Herbs You Must Have in an Herb Garden

By Morris
Father of Ruby, assistant to Garron

Herbs are strange, mysterious things: sometimes they can save your life; sometimes they can take it. There are those in our kingdom who likely use, occasionally, herbs to take a life, but I prefer to save lives with them. My herbs are used by the village Healer in Fairendale for all manner of afflictions, as were the herbs of my ancestors. Our family has always contained skillful herbalists who work closely with both the village gardener, to produce an herb garden, and the village Healer, to produce effective remedies and cures.

I recommend that everyone—young and old—have their own small or large herb garden. Herbs are useful for seasoning meals, healing wounds, summoning sleep, and reducing anxiety and melancholy, among many other uses. If you have been a victim of an intentional or unintentional poisoning, herbs can even induce your stomach to extract the poison (I'm speaking here of foxglove, which must come with a warning: foxglove is highly potent, and only a tiny fraction of it need be consumed to induce vomiting; if you consume too much, you will likely die anyway).

It is best for the amateur herbalist to grow simple yet

robust plants that might be used in teas, poultices, powders, and infusions.

Here are some plants you might want in your herb garden:

Aloe vera

The clear pulp of the aloe vera leaf can be used to heal minor cuts and burns and even eliminate some skin problems, such as the red bumps that sometimes afflict the faces of those between the ages of twelve and nineteen. The apothecary sells salves in his shop, which he says can smooth the appearance of anyone's skin. And his claims seem to be true.

You can also eat the leaf pulp to prevent digestive problems.

Peppermint

Chewing on a leaf of peppermint can give you the kind of fresh breath you want when talking to that special person who secretly makes your heart dance. My daughter is too young to know this feeling. She will be too young for the next seventeen years, until she is approximately twenty-nine. Perhaps thirty. But if you happen to be someone else's son or daughter, peppermint is a wonderful breath freshener.

Sniffing the leaves of peppermint can also prevent vomiting and nausea. This is helpful if you happen to be riding a horse and the lurching motion of the horse causes nausea.

A poultice made from peppermint can relieve headaches and muscle cramps.

Thyme

Thyme is a power herb that can be used for all sorts of colds, illnesses, and respiratory problems. Heat it as a gargle for problems with the throat. Crush the leaves and apply them to the neck to reduce throat infections.

If brewed in a tea, thyme can relieve congestion of the chest, rattling coughs, and breathing ailments. With a bit of honey, even children will enjoy this remedy.

Rosemary

In the ancient days, rosemary was used for potions, the ancient form of sorcery. Rosemary could induce people to remember, so it was used in both Remembering spells and Truth spells. Today, the plant can be used for general wellbeing, particularly for the brain and memory function.

Chamomile

The flower heads of this plant can be made into a soothing tea. To make a cup of chamomile tea, take a handful of flowers, sprinkle them in a bowl, and pour over them boiling water. Let them steep for a quarter of an hour. The tea is helpful when you feel anxious, nervous, or wide awake when you should be sleeping.

Sage

Sage is a marvelous herb that can prevent flatulence, particularly when used in cooking. If you are prone to flatulence, you must keep sage around; it is not considered polite to flatulate in the company of others, though, at times, it is completely uncontrollable and unavoidable.

Inhaling sage can also provide relief for respiratory problems, perhaps especially those caused by being exposed to another's flatulence.

Lavender

A lovely purple-tinted flower, lavender effectively relieves headaches and melancholy. You can place some dried flowers under a pillow, if you are fortunate enough to have a pillow, to get a more relaxed sleep. The herb can also accelerate wound healing.

Echinacea

This miraculous herb helps the body fight bacterial and viral infections. The plant's roots can be used to treat wounds, burns, insect bites, and even snake bites. The flower buds can be used to treat colds and other illnesses.

It is a powerful herb to have around.

In your quest to cultivate the perfect herb garden, remember: all things in moderation. If you find that any of these herbs interfere with your normal ability to function—as in, say, causing you to itch all over or break out into unexplainable red splotches or flatulate more violently than you typically flatulate, discontinue their use immediately.

But, I believe, every person can benefit from a little

herbal healing.

How to Find an Invisible Tower

By Prince Cole
Prince of Rosehaven

I am certainly trying. I will let you know when I succeed.

For now, I have only this: Never give up.

The Royal Family of Fairendale

King Willis: The current king of Fairendale. Son of King Sebastien. Has a deep love for sweet rolls.

Queen Clarion: The current queen of Fairendale. Is underestimated by her husband, but she will prove just how powerful she is in due time.

Prince Virgil: Son of King Willis and Queen Clarion, best friend of Theo. Prefers rye bread with melted butter to sweet rolls, depending on the day.

King Sebastien: Deceased king of Fairendale, exception to the line of boys who tried to steal thrones and were, upon failing at their quest, forever banished. Was killed by a blackbird.

The Former Royal Family of Fairendale

The Good King Brendon: Former king of Fairendale responsible for the alliance between the people of Fairendale and the dragons of Morad, lost the throne when it was stolen by King Sebastien. Killed in the Great Battle.

Queen Marion: Wife of the Good King Brendon, died mysteriously when her daughter was very young. Now lives in Lincastle and is "affectionately" called the

Evil Queen.

Princess Maren: Daughter of the Good King Brendon and Queen Marion. She has been missing since the Great Battle.

The Villagers of Fairendale

Arthur: Village furniture maker and magic instructor to girls who possess the gift of magic in the village of Fairendale. Is a bit reckless but always manages to come out on the other side—though one is not always assured it will be so.

Maude: Arthur's wife. Bakes spectacular pumpkin spice sugar cookies. Prefers caution to reckless abandon.

Hazel: Daughter of Arthur and Maude, twin of Theo. Cares for the village sheep and can even, amazingly, understand them. 12 years old.

Theo: Son of Arthur and Maude, twin of Hazel. Finishes his chores early so he can sit in on magic lessons. 12 years old.

Mercy: Daughter of Cora, best friend of Hazel. Prefers spectacular acts of magic to "boring" ones.

Cora: Mother of Mercy, widow, shape shifter. A woman who moves. Unofficial leader of the villagers in Fairendale.

Garron: The town gardener. Talks to plants as though they can hear him.

Bertie: The town baker. Enjoys showing off his air-kneading skills for the children. Or used to.

Staff of Fairendale Castle

Garth: Page for King Willis, the oldest of twelve children. Sometimes calls King Willis "Your Wideness" when he is feeling particularly prickly.

Cook: One of the few shape shifters in the land. Shape shifts into a bear. Is highly annoyed by her assistant, Calvin.

Calvin: An orphan who began working as Cook's assistant instead of traveling to live with distant relatives in Ashvale—and so did not perish in the Fire Mountain that claimed the entire population of Ashvale many years ago. Tasked with feeding the prisoners in the dungeons beneath the dungeons.

Sir Greyson: Captain of the king's guard. Receives medicine, which keeps his mother alive, for his service to the king. Carries a magical sword that cannot be lifted by any but him.

Sir Merrick: Second in command to Sir Greyson. Has a blind daughter named Agnes.

Gus, Timmy, Florence: Three blind, talking mice. Not technically staff of the castle, but they roam about it unseen, gathering information. It is suggested they were once people, transformed by a spell.

Important Prophets

Aleen: Prophetess who is one hundred forty-two years old, from the kingdom of White Wind. Wears ebony skin and what appears to be snakes for hair (though it is not). Sacrificed her life to change the fate of the Fairendale children in Book 6.

Yerin: Prophet who is one hundred forty-two years old, from the wild woodland between Lincastle and Eastermoor. Has white hair that makes the dark of the dungeons where he is imprisoned a bit less dark.

Folen: Former prophet of Lincastle, father of Iddo. Trapped in a looking glass created by Queen Marion. It was left on the grounds of Fairendale, just before the Great Battle.

Iddo: Prophet of Lincastle, son of Folen. Trained King Sebastien in both dark and light magic, though he is more scientist than sorcerer. Created a machine that can bring the dead to life again. It has only worked once.

Bregdon: Prophet of White Wind. Most powerful

prophet in the land, known as the Old Man. Wrote and enchanted the Old Man's Great Book. Brought Queen Marion and the three Graces back to life. Has mysteriously disappeared.

Dragons of Morad

Zorag: King of the dragons of Morad. Wears green scales with an ivory belly. Lost his parents in the Great Battle, when King Sebastien stole the throne from the Good King Brendon. Would like nothing more than peace.

Blindell: Zorag's cousin, raised as the dragon king's son. Wears black scales and spikes all down his back. Lost his parents in the Great Battle, when King Sebastien stole the throne from the Good King Brendon. Would like nothing more than revenge.

Larus: One of the elder dragons of Morad, male. Counselor to Zorag. Wears blue-green scales that shimmer like water. Has a green horn on the top of his snout.

Malera: One of the elder dragons of Morad, female. Counselor to Zorag. Wears bright red scales and an ivory belly.

Alvah: One of the elder dragons of Morad, female.

Counselor to Zorag. Ancient dragon who has been alive since before Zorag's father was born. Wears orange scales that used to be red but have faded in time.

Oned: One of the elder dragons of Morad, male. Counselor to Zorag. So ancient he is gray, colorless, with scales peeled off in places.

Kohar: Ancient food gatherer for the dragons of Morad, male. Wears pale yellow scales.

Other Important Dragons

Rezedron: King of the dragons of Eyre, uncle of Zorag. Dying of wounds sustained from a poisonous rose in Rosehaven, believed to be dark magic.

Residents of the Violet Sea

Arya: Twelfth daughter of King Tritanius, who rules the Violet Sea. Adventurous, impulsive, often considered rebellious by her father. Saves the Huntsman from death by fairy magic. Loves a mortal.

Other Important Characters

The Graces: Formerly mortal women who died and

were brought back to eternal life by the Old Man. Now known as Splendor, Good Cheer, and Mirth, or, collectively, the Graces. Maintain the balance of good and evil in the realm. Cannot predict the future.

The Grim Reaper: Master of the dead. Leads an army of Black-Eyed Beings. Longs to be seen as something more than a passing shadow.

Yasmin: Frankenstein-like creature brought back to life by the scientific tools of Iddo. Formerly known as Gladys, mother of Sebastien, before he stole the throne of Fairendale.

The lost 12-year-old children of Fairendale

Ursula

Chester

Charles

Thumbelina (known as Lina among the children)

Minnie

Jasper: Transported to the land of White Wind by Hazel's Vanishing spell. Becomes a wolf who befriends a girl in a red cloak. Runs very fast.

Frederick

Ruby: Transported to the land of Rosehaven by

Hazel's Vanishing spell. Becomes an old woman who meets Rapunzel, befriends her, and supplies her with chamomile. She is a masterful gardener.

Martin

Oscar

Homer: Transported to the land of Rosehaven by Hazel's Vanishing spell. Becomes a dwarf who can spin straw into gold, otherwise known as Rumpelstiltskin.

Anna: Transported to the land of Eastermoor by Hazel's Vanishing spell. Becomes an old, bent woman who resides in the Were Woods. Is awkward with magic, which causes some unexpected problems.

Aurora

Rose

Edgar

Harriet (known as Hattie among the children)

Isabel (known as Izzy among the children)

Ralph

Dorothy

Julian

Tom Thumb

Philip: Transported to the forest outside Lincastle by Hazel's Vanishing spell. Becomes the leader of the Merry Men, otherwise known as Robin Hood. Can shoot an arrow straight to the target, even if the arrow is crooked.

Other lost children of Fairendale

August: One of the lost boys of Fairendale, escaped with Theo. Known as the leader of the lost boys. Resides in a rundown shelter in Lincastle. 11 years old.

Leopold: One of the lost boys of Fairendale, escaped with Theo. Resides with August and the other lost boys. 11 years old.

Fineas: One of the lost boys of Fairendale, escaped with Theo. Resides with August and the other lost boys. 11 years old.

Norman: One of the lost boys of Fairendale, escaped with Theo. Resides with August and the other lost boys. 10 years old.

Henry: One of the lost boys of Fairendale, escaped with Theo. Resides with August and the other lost boys. 10 years old.

Ernest: One of the lost boys of Fairendale, escaped with Theo. Resides with August and the other lost boys. 10 years old.

Agnes: Daughter of Sir Merrick, trapped in the dungeons beneath the dungeons of Fairendale castle. Blind, but quite good at hearing and sensing what others cannot.

About the Author

Though she has never successfully grown an elaborate garden (she blames the South Texas heat and the large black squirrel that stole into her yard when she last attempted a garden and left her a handful of half-eaten offerings of cucumbers and squash), L.R. enjoys the fruits of gardens—especially tomatoes, cucumbers, and blackberries. She secretly hopes that one of her sons will exhibit signs of being a "Ruby"—as in, a person with a green thumb, rather than someone with a slightly burnt-hued thumb.

And just because she has not yet had a successful gardening year in her sadly desert-like garden does not mean L.R. has quit trying. She believes that to succeed in anything, one must try, try, and, when the world is whispering *quit*, try again. You never know which try will succeed. (She tells her sons this often, especially when they are "trying" to tie their shoes, which is to say they are staring at their laces announcing they cannot do it today.)

When she is not urging her children to try again and they are not complaining about how she always tells them to try again, L.R. and her family can be found reading stories together, drinking chamomile tea together, and eating a hearty dinner together around their table.

L.R. is the queen of her castle in San Antonio, Texas, where she lives with her king and six young princes, who almost always try hard. Especially when it comes to eating. She tries hard, too. In spite of the wild cacophony that daily grips her home, she still manages to write thousands of words for her fiction stories, essays, and poetry every week.

www.lrpatton.com

A Note From L.R.

Dear Reader,

I sincerely hope you have enjoyed this telling of how Rapunzel was *really* locked inside her tower. When we only listen to one side of a story, what often happens is we believe only a partial truth. For many years I (and you, perhaps) believed that Rapunzel was imprisoned by an evil sorceress, when, in reality, her situation was orchestrated by a sorceress, yes, but one who happened to be a twelve-year-old girl and who also happened to be attempting to protect her friend from the dangers of the world.

Every encounter with another human being is an opportunity to hear someone's story. Remember that as you walk through your days.

This is how we love. This is how we are loved. We listen, and we are listened to.

I write for children because I want them to feel seen and heard. I want to re-tell their villainous (or not-so-villainous) stories so that they know they do not have to be perfect to be loved.

We are loved no matter what.

And that is something grand and wonderful.

Every book I write, regardless of whether it is part of

the Fairendale series or it is some other imaginative tale, is written to

- Empower readers with hope, love, joy, peace, knowledge, and the necessary tools to make a better tomorrow
- Ensure that readers fall in love and stay in love with reading
- Foster in readers a love of language
- Encourage families to bond around meaningful stories
- Show readers characters who look like them
- Matter to the wider world.

I believe in the power of stories. I believe that stories have the power to inspire, inform, spread love, and effect real change in the lives of readers. And I write every book with this higher purpose in mind.

Though my writing is done alone, my world-changing is not. I need readers like you to help get my books into the hands of those who don't yet know the hope and inspiration that can be found in them. So here are some ways you can help:

1. Leave a review on Amazon.

Reviews help other readers find my books. The more readers who find my book, the better able I am to accomplish what I've listed above.

2. Tell your friends about this book.

Word of mouth is one of the most powerful tools we have for sharing the things we love—and it is, consequently, one of the most powerful tools I have for sharing my work with new readers.

I appreciate anything you can do to help my books get into the hands of readers and help create a literacy movement that matters.

My princes are in need of mediation (during which I will listen to both sides of their story and likely still not come to a conclusive conclusion), so I must bid you farewell. In the future, please stop by my web site to say hello, to access some really fun bonus materials, or, perhaps, both.

In love,

L.R.

Acknowledgements

It does not require much imagination to know and understand that a book takes many people to unfold into existence. There are so many who inspire, direct, and walk beside me on my journey. Here are a few:

Ben, who takes my demands in stride, creating fabulous covers, drawing ridiculously beautiful maps, and, most valuably, telling me to calm down when I'm getting a little out of hand

My sons, whose requests for the next Fairendale stories spur my writing

My launch team members, who are always ready to read another of my books

My mom, who obviously doesn't understand how long it takes to write a book in an epic series like this (love you, Mom!)

Folklorists, who have left their tales for authors like me to reimagine and retell.

Thank you, thank you, thank you.

Enjoy more stories from the magical Fairendale series:

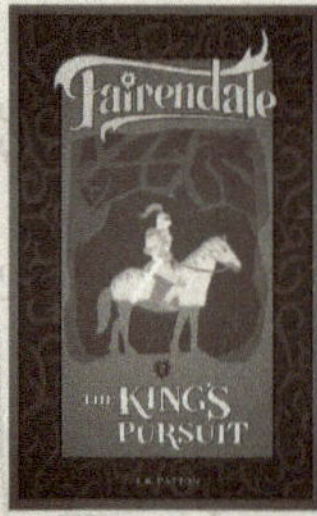

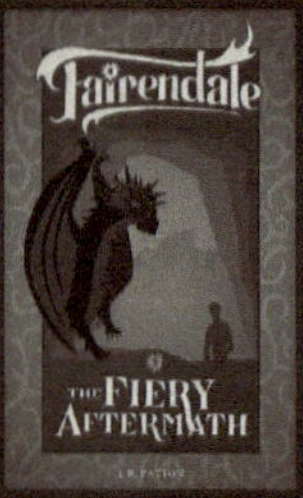

LRPatton.com/Fairendale

Starter Library

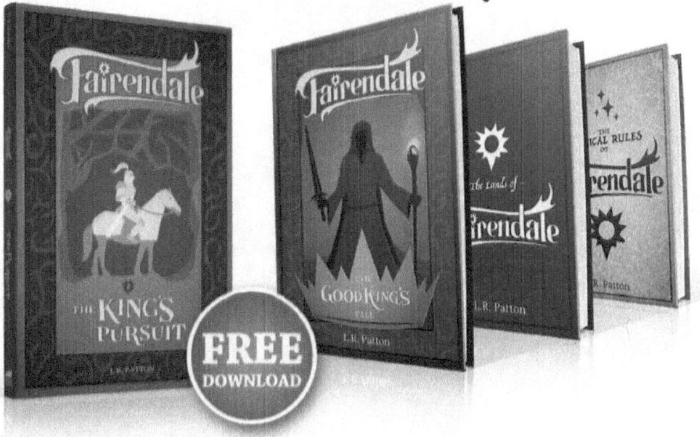

A singular obsession. A safe hiding space. A never-ending search.

The king's guard has been searching all the lands of the realm for the missing Fairendale children. But, alas, Captain Sir Greyson has returned, after many days, to report to King Willis that no children have been found. The king, quite angry at this disappointing news, orders another search, this one closer to home—right inside the dangerous Weeping Woods.

*Continue your journey into the world of Fairendale with Book 2: The King's Pursuit, a short story prequel, "The Good King's Fall" and some important bonus material, **free for a limited time.***

To get your FREE bonus materials, visit *
LRPatton.com/goodking

*Must be 13 or older to be eligible

www.ingramcontent.com/pod-product-compliance
Lightning Source LLC
Chambersburg PA
CBHW050613190726
48283CB00007B/2405